Sound the
Jubilee

Sound the
Jubilee

SANDRA FORRESTER

Lodestar Books

DUTTON / NEW YORK

*This book is dedicated with love and thanks
to my mother and father,
Dorothy Fine Forrester and Robert Martin Forrester,
for caring and believing.*

*And to Dave, who wanted to make a difference.
And did.*

Library of Congress Cataloging-in-Publication Data
Forrester, Sandra.
Sound the jubilee / Sandra Forrester.—1st ed.
p.   cm.
Summary: A slave and her family find refuge on Roanoke
Island, North Carolina, during the Civil War.
ISBN 0-525-67468-1
[1. Slavery—Fiction.   2. Roanoke Island (N.C.)—History—
Fiction.   3. United States—History—Civil War, 1861–1865—
Fiction.]   I. Title.
PZ7.F7717So   1995
[Fic]—dc20   94-32664
                                                      CIP
                                                       AC

Published in the United States by Lodestar Books,
an affiliate of Dutton Children's Books,
a division of Penguin Books USA Inc.,
375 Hudson Street, New York, New York 10014

Published simultaneously in Canada
by McClelland & Stewart, Toronto

Editor: Rosemary Brosnan   Designer: Richard Granald
Printed in the U.S.A.   First Edition
10   9   8   7   6   5   4

Preface

The string of islands known as the Outer Banks hugs the North Carolina coast for 175 miles, acting as a natural buffer between the sometimes fierce Atlantic Ocean and the mainland. Even though development has been extensive in the last half century, it is still easy to imagine "the Banks" as they were during the Civil War—before the forests at Nags Head were cleared for construction, before erosion shifted mountains of sand from one site to another—because the essential character of these barrier islands remains unchanged.

This is a land that has battled—and not always won—an ongoing war against nature. Nothing fragile can survive the hurricanes that come each summer and autumn, the savage nor'easters that blow in winter, the treacherous and ever-changing underwater sandbars that have earned the Banks the nickname "Graveyard of the Atlantic."

Before the Civil War, Nags Head was a popular resort for wealthy Carolinians, a pleasant and healthy escape from summer fevers on the inland plantations. But when the war began in April 1861, the Outer Banks took on a more important role. Both the Union and Confederate armies knew that dominion over these islands meant control of a major maritime supply route to northeastern North Carolina, Norfolk, Virginia, and the Chesapeake

Bay. The South held on to the Banks until August 1861, when a joint campaign by the Union army and navy resulted in the capture of Forts Clark and Hatteras at Hatteras Inlet. In February 1862, Roanoke Island was captured by the North, and held until the end of the war.

Blacks fleeing from slavery began to arrive on Roanoke Island immediately following the battle. Eventually they numbered over three thousand. Many of these self-freed slaves found employment with the Union army—building a fort and docks, and working for the quartermaster and commissary corps. Some had skills that allowed them to become self-employed. Others served in the army when blacks were recruited for the first time in 1863.

In May 1863, the U.S. government granted the Roanoke Island community formal status, assigning land to the former slaves who lived there and beginning to educate them for life in a free society after the war ended. The island's new residents built houses, planted gardens, and proceeded to live rather ordinary lives under extraordinary circumstances.

The principal characters in this novel—Titus, Ella, Angeline, Maddie, and Pride—are all fictional. But the military generals and Miss Elizabeth James actually lived during these times and played roles in history as depicted herein. To the best of my knowledge, there was no River Bend Plantation in North Carolina, but there were many cotton plantations like it throughout the South.

The songs included here are spirituals and work songs that slaves created to voice the grief, the despair—and the triumph—they experienced in their daily lives. These Sorrow Songs, as they are called, speak with haunting eloquence of a people's longing to be free.

The Roanoke Island community was not the U.S. government's only attempt to provide sanctuary to former slaves. But owing to its size, its isolation from the war-torn South, its sophisticated social structure, and its duration, the settlement on Roanoke Island was a unique phenomenon in this country's history.

Sadly, the three thousand men, women, and children who risked their lives for freedom, and who created the largest and most prosperous community on the Outer Banks up to that time, are mentioned only briefly—if at all—in history books. There is no marker on Roanoke Island to show us where the settlement stood. But these people's brave struggle deserves to be remembered. And their determination serves as an example for us all.

PART ONE

River Bend Plantation

AUGUST 1861–JANUARY 1862

One

The Master and the Mistress were in mourning. Their older boy Jamie, named James Edward McCartha after his father, had died of typhoid fever just six weeks after riding off with his brother to fight in the war.

Since the young Master's death, an unsettling silence had descended on River Bend Plantation—for when the Master and Mistress grieved, everyone grieved. The slaves were now forbidden to sing as they walked to and from the fields each day. And the house servants had been ordered to remove their shoes when passing the Mistress's closed door.

Taking off her shoes was no hardship for Maddie. The high-topped leather footgear was a nuisance as far as she was concerned. Sometimes she wished she worked in the fields, with her toes wiggling free in the rich North Carolina soil. She knew Elsie and Ben and the others worked hard, planting and hoeing and picking the cotton that kept the plantation going. But at least they were out in the sunshine where they could talk and laugh—not locked up in the dark, silent house with the grieving Mistress.

Maddie moved her dust cloth slowly along the spines of the Master's books. Cleaning the library was the one chore she loved, because it allowed her to look at—to actually *touch!*—the beautiful volumes.

She scanned the names on the spines. Gibbon, Hume, Johnson, Voltaire—names she had never heard before and wasn't even sure how to pronounce. What did these people have to say that would fill a whole book? This one called *The Works of Thomas Paine,* and the many others by a man named William Shakespeare—what were *they* about? Had the Master read them all, from front cover to back? If the books were hers, she'd read every precious word, Maddie thought, not recognizing the pang of envy she felt for what it was.

Her sister, Angeline, laughed at Maddie when she described, almost reverently, the rich colors of the bindings and the softness of the leather. But her mama grew stern when Maddie mentioned the books.

"Mistress broke the law teachin' me to read, and I done the same teachin' you and Angeline," Ella said with hard black eyes. "But we do that in private, daughter, you hear? Don't you let me catch you readin' them books. Even Mistress couldn't stop Master from whoopin' you good if he caught you stealin' one. You hear me, girl?"

"Yes, Mama," Maddie always replied meekly. But she still felt a delicious thrill whenever she entered this room and imagined what it would be like if she *could* pick up one of the wondrous books and read it.

Maddie had turned eleven that past spring and was now expected to carry the load of a woman. Angeline, who was two years older, had been the perfect housemaid since she was nine. Mistress never seemed to tire of praising Angeline for her cheerfulness and obedience.

Maddie had always known she would never measure up to her sister. Angeline had been born with a sweet temperament and a desire to please that endeared her to

4

everybody, from the Mistress to the field workers. It was obvious that Angeline was Mama's favorite, just as Baby Pride, the only son to survive past infancy, was Papa's. Maddie was nobody's favorite.

Mama lost patience with Maddie's woolgathering, and with her tendency to leave a chore half finished in favor of slipping off to feed the stable cats or meet Papa when he led the workers in from the fields. Mistress complained often to Ella about her younger daughter's insolence, which meant that Maddie hadn't lowered her eyes and curtsied when addressed, or had tried to explain why a chore wasn't done.

"Slaves don't explain nothin'," Ella told her over and over. "Master and Mistress don't care *why* it's not done, they just care that it's *not*. You got to try harder, Maddie, like Angeline. See how she smiles at Mistress? But sweetly, not lookin' her straight in the face. Do like Angeline."

So Maddie tried. She really did want to please Mama and make Papa proud of her. After one of Mama's tongue-lashings, she'd go about her chores with a vigor that amazed everybody. For a day or two, she'd rise before anybody else and have the fires in the Big House blazing before Mama and Angeline arrived. She'd carry water without spilling it, gather eggs without breaking them, and curtsy prettily whenever she was within ten feet of Mistress.

But then she'd see a rainbow in the garden—the Devil's Garter, Aunt Lucy called it—or hear Papa's deep laugh as he passed the house with the field hands. And before she had time to think about it, she'd be out of the house, running like a spindle-shanked colt to freedom!

Once, when Mama was fussing at her for not trying hard enough, Papa had pulled her onto his lap—even though she was way too big for that—and remarked that

Maddie was a lot like him: restless and troublesome, but smart as a whip.

"Too smart for her own good," Mama had said sharply. And Papa had winked at Maddie, letting her know that he understood the need to break loose now and again. She might not be his favorite, but she knew she was special to him, even if she wasn't a son. Or beautiful like Angeline.

Maddie and Pride took after Papa, with their angular, long-limbed bodies and complexions the color of hickory nuts, while Angeline was small and rounded like Mama. Angeline had Mama's high cheekbones and the slanting black eyes that showed up so pretty against her honey-gold skin. Maddie had figured out long ago that Mistress would like her a whole lot better if her skin was light like Angeline's and Mama's.

Maddie turned reluctantly from the bookshelves and began to dust the Master's desk. This was the tedious part, so she saved it for last. The desk was covered with paperweights, inkwells, and papers that had to be lifted and then returned to exactly the right spot. Master went into a temper if he found anything moved even the slightest bit from where he'd left it.

Today there was even more disorder than usual. Master had left the big brown book he called *The Plantation Journal* open on the desk with stacks of papers all around it.

Maddie had no interest in the journal. She wouldn't have given it a second glance if she hadn't caught sight of her papa's name printed in neat black letters near the top of the page:

Titus, about 36 years, $1,000

the entry read. Below this were the names of other workers at River Bend. Above the list the Master had penned:

SLAVES ON THE PLANTATION OF JAMES EDWARD
McCARTHA, AND THEIR APPROXIMATE WORTH.

Maddie was curious to see if her own name was written in the book. But the sound of a door opening in the hall startled her into remembering how vexed Mama would be with her for prying into Master's business. So she dusted the journal without bothering to lift it and hurried from the library.

It was time to shell peas for supper, even though it seemed a waste for Mama to fix big meals, with the Mistress not eating and the Master away most of the time.

"I do it 'cause I'm told to," Ella had snapped when Maddie voiced her opinion. "And you'd do well to follow the example."

Luther, the houseman, was talking to Mama and Angeline when Maddie came into the kitchen. Luther was probably the oldest slave on the plantation except for Aunt Lucy, and the most trusted. Even though he was moving slower every year, and woke each morning with his old joints paining him more, Luther ruled the Big House with an authority that nobody questioned.

"You remember to sweep the porch?" Ella asked when she saw Maddie.

"Yes, Mama."

"And dust the front parlor?"

"Yes'm."

"Sounds like you been right busy, Maddie girl." Luther gave her his slow, kind smile.

"She'll make up for it tomorrow," Ella declared, but her tone was less cross.

Angeline, who was rolling out dough for biscuits, looked up. "What with Aunt Lucy feelin' poorly all week,

I don't know how we'd of managed Pride without Maddie."

Maddie flashed her sister a look of gratitude.

"There's a basket'a peas waitin' for you in the pantry," Ella told her, and Maddie retreated to the little room off the kitchen to shell them.

A few minutes later Maddie heard Nancy, Mistress's personal maid, greet Mama, Angeline, and Luther. Nancy had a sharp tongue that Mistress never suspected, since Nancy spoke sweet as sorghum molasses in front of the white folks. But with the other servants, she was quick to speak her mind. Maddie didn't like her much, but Angeline said Nancy had the hardest job of any of them, so Maddie kept her feelings to herself.

"Mistress done 'cided to git up for supper," Nancy said in that nasty tone she reserved for the servants' ears. "I s'pose even a grievin' mama cain't take to her bed forever."

"Mistress done suffered a powerful loss," Luther reminded her. "Death ain't easy whether it come to the Big House or the cabin."

"She still got young Master Andrew off fightin' the Yankees," Nancy retorted. "Still plenty'a McCartha men to see we stays slaves forever."

"You know I don't like that kind'a talk in my kitchen," Mama said.

"Don't be such a scairt rabbit, Ella." Nancy's voice was hard. "What you say to that man'a yours when he go to slave row ever' night to talk about the war? If Master catches 'em meetin' and plottin' in the cabins, there'll be trouble for sho'. And his foreman the ringleader of it."

"Titus goes to the cabins to visit with his friends," Ella

said coldly. "And I'll thank you to curb your tongue on things you don't know."

"I know plenty about the talk in the cabins," Nancy replied slyly. "I'm there most nights myself, when I kin slip off from Mistress. That sleepin' draft the doc give her sho' do help. I just double the dose and she's dead to the world in no time."

"Nancy!" This was Luther's voice, gruff with shock and anger.

"It don't hurt her none," Nancy said crossly. "Gives me a few hours to myself is all. Ain't I earned that much, after puttin' up with her airs and temper all these years?"

"Girl, you askin' for trouble," Luther warned her. "If Mistress ever hear you talkin' like this, she'll send you to the fields for sho'. Maybe even sell you to the slave traders."

"Oh, no, not our good kind Mistress," Nancy mocked him. "How many times you hear her say, 'We don't sells our people here at River Bend. They's fam'ly, and you don't sells fam'ly.' "

"If she hears you talkin' like this, she may change her mind," Ella said. "You just think on it, Nancy, there's folks have it harder'n us."

"We's still slaves, ain't we?" Nancy demanded.

"Slaves with warm beds and full bellies," Ella said. "And I know my babies won't be sold right outta my arms."

"But we's still slaves," Nancy repeated softly. And Maddie thought she sounded like she might cry.

Two

It was long after dark when Maddie followed Ella and Angeline to the detached kitchen quarter where they lived. Inside the frame building was a big room with a cavernous fireplace. Aunt Lucy, whose wizened old face resembled a dried crabapple, was sitting in a rocker by the hearth with Pride in her arms.

"Titus not come in yet?" Ella stooped to check on her sleeping son.

"You knows they won't be back till they picks their two hundred pounds," Aunt Lucy said.

Ella nodded. During cotton-picking season she was used to seeing little of her husband. As foreman of the field workers, he had to stay in the fields until the last slave picked the day's quota and weighed in at the gin house.

"Mama, you rest. I'll warm the food." Angeline was already unloading the basket of leftovers from supper at the Big House. "Aunt Lucy, how does chicken and spoon bread sound?"

"Mighty fine, chile," the old woman replied agreeably, as she always did.

Aunt Lucy wasn't blood kin, but they were proud to share their quarters with her. Unlike Ella and Titus and their children, Lucy hadn't been born at River Bend. She had had many masters, and been sold many times, before finally making her way to the plantation in North Carolina. The scars on her back affirmed that not all her masters had treated her kindly.

For twenty years, Aunt Lucy had birthed the babies and nursed the ills of slaves at River Bend. Now that she was too crippled to move around much, she sent Maddie into the woods to gather the herbs and roots she needed for her healing potions. In the beginning, Maddie hadn't been very interested in the old woman's doctoring. But lately she found herself really watching Aunt Lucy as she worked, fascinated by the way Aunt Lucy turned the strange-smelling weeds into healing brews—as if by magic.

Ella lifted Pride from Aunt Lucy's arms and sat down with him in another rocker by the fire. He was big for two, handsome like his papa—and strong. That was the important part. After losing three little boys before their first birthdays, Ella was forever studying her son for signs of ill health.

"Maddie, you set the table," Angeline said as she pulled out the big iron cooking pot.

Like everything else in the room, the dishes were from the Big House. That was one of the privileges Ella enjoyed as a house servant, the chance to see that her family lived better than the slaves in the cabins. Of course, the dishes were cracked—destined for the dustbin when Ella retrieved them—but they were serviceable.

The big room was where the family cooked and took their meals and gathered in the evenings to sew and talk and read from the Bible. After the supper dishes were washed and put away, Angeline and Maddie did their lessons at the table. Each night Ella gave them passages to read from the Bible and sums to do. Unlike Angeline, who showed no special interest in reading and ciphering, Maddie looked forward to the lessons. She loved holding the heavy Bible in her lap and sounding out the words in it. Sums weren't as much fun as reading, but she worked hard at those too. She secretly hoped someday she could teach the children in the cabins to read and cipher.

The family slept in three small closets off the main room. Aunt Lucy had earned the right to her own room and bed. Ella and Titus shared the bed in the second room, with Pride sleeping on a pallet beside them. And Angeline and Maddie slept in the third room on a thick mattress filled with cotton.

Mama had brought patched sheets from the Big House that Mistress had said to use for rags. On cold winter evenings, Mama and Angeline made quilts for the beds with scraps of cloth they had saved. Maddie felt a twinge of guilt when she thought of the thin mattresses and ragged blankets used by the slaves on slave row. Nobody on the row had a thick quilt to snuggle under when the winter winds blew.

They waited to eat until Papa got in. He looked tired, but he still had a hug for Maddie and Angeline, and a smile for the rest of them. After supper he held Pride on his knee and played silly games that made the boy crow with laughter.

Maddie and Angeline were doing their lessons while Mama made corn cakes for Papa to take to the fields the next day. He could have had food and sweet milk from the Big House, but he chose to eat the same dinner as the other field slaves—corn cakes, cold bacon, and water.

"B'lieve I'll walk down to the cabins later on." He said

it casually, as he always did, but Maddie could feel her mama tense up at his words.

"I was hopin' you'd stay in tonight," Ella said softly. She was pouring water into a bowl of cornmeal, her back to them as she worked.

"I could use a breath'a air."

"But Master says no meetin' in the cabins after dark—"

"Ella, we done talked about this." He spoke quietly, but Maddie knew the tone. His mind was set.

Angeline's head was bent over the piece of paper on which Mama had written columns of figures. As usual, it was taking her longer than Maddie to finish. Maddie pretended to read from the Bible as she watched Mama and Papa through lowered lashes. She had never known them to disagree, had never even thought about the possibility of an argument between them. But she knew now they *were* disagreeing, and it made her uneasy. Maybe because Nancy had said Papa could get in trouble going to the cabins, or because she could sense her mama's fear.

"The bluecoats is gettin' closer ever' day," Titus said gently. "Only a matter'a time till they gets here and sets us free."

"Mistress says they're nothin' but devils." Ella turned to face him, and Maddie could see the fear on her face. Ella opened her mouth to say more, then noticed that Maddie was watching her. She turned back abruptly to the corn cakes.

Maddie lay awake a long time after she and Angeline were in bed. She wanted to be awake when Papa came back, to make sure he was all right before she went to sleep.

It was very late when she heard him come in. Even so, Mama was waiting up.

"You should be asleep," Maddie heard him say.

"You were gone a long time."

"Don't be scared for me." Maddie thought he sounded angry.

"Somebody's gotta be," Mama said sharply. "Don't you know the risk? And for what! A lot'a nonsense dreams of freedom."

"It ain't nonsense, Ella."

Maddie had never heard her papa sound so cold. Her uneasiness grew.

"Your friends think the bluecoats is gonna march in here and hand 'em their precious freedom?" Mama demanded. "Another kind'a slavery's more like it, a harsher kind. Mistress says they'll burn the Big House to the ground. Steal our animals, strip our fields. And take us North to do their work. She says they'll harness us to plows like mules—"

"Ella, hush up!"

There was a long, dreadful silence. Maddie lay there holding her breath, listening to the steady *thump-thump-thump* of her heart. Then her papa said, more softly, "The woman tells you that 'cause she's scared. She don't want us runnin' off North 'cause they couldn't keep this place goin' without us."

"Mistress been good to us, Titus."

"Mistress takes good care'a her property," Papa said bitterly. "But I don't want to be owned no more. Don't want nobody ownin' my children—or my wife. There's some in the cabins ready to run—"

"I won't listen!"

"Old Shad and Caleb's got theirselves a plan. They hid one'a Master's rifles—"

"Don't tell me, Titus! I don't wanta know."

14

There was silence again, and then Ella said, so softly that Maddie had to strain to hear her, "I don't think I wanta be free if it means leavin' my home."

"River Bend's not your home." Papa's voice was kind again. "It's the Master's and Mistress's home. We're just stock, like the horses. No more'n that."

Three

I t was Sunday morning. Maddie was racing through her chores in the kitchen quarter with a speed that would have astounded her family had they been there to see it. Even though it was still dark outside, Ella and Angeline had already left for the kitchen in the Big House.

"You sho' you got that pan clean?" Aunt Lucy queried from her chair beside the fire. "You done them dishes mighty fast."

"Clean as can be." Maddie held up the old skillet for the woman's inspection. "All I got left's sweepin' and feedin' the chickens."

"What you in such an all-fired hurry for, girl?" Aunt Lucy asked. She was watching Pride play on the floor with a wooden top Titus had made for him.

"Papa says I can help hand out rations when I finish my chores." Maddie reached for the old straw broom.

"Sweep up, then you kin go. I'll take Pride to feed the chickens."

"You sure?" Maddie stopped her furious sweeping to look at Aunt Lucy. "You feel up to goin' outside?"

"My old bones don't pain me so much today," Aunt Lucy assured her. " 'Sides, them hens ain't been layin' like they should. Time I give 'em some nettle leaves with their feed."

Ten minutes later Maddie was racing around the kitchen garden toward the smokehouse. The sun was just beginning to come up over the trees, but already the slaves had gathered for their weekly rations.

Some of the women and children called out to Maddie, and she waved in return. It was just as well that Ella wasn't there to see the friendly exchange between her daughter and the field hands. Like the Mistress, Ella believed that house servants had no business mingling with the slaves from the cabins. She had no idea how often Maddie and Titus went to slave row on Sunday afternoons to visit their friends.

Titus was standing on the steps of the smokehouse when he saw Maddie. "Just in time, daughter." He handed her a ring of keys. "You unlock the door while I sets up the scales."

Maddie's dark eyes grew big. "Really, Papa?" Mama, Papa, and Luther were the only slaves on the plantation allowed to carry the keys, and now Papa was entrusting them to her. Maddie felt proud and nervous as Papa helped her find the right key.

After she had unlocked the smokehouse door, Papa brought out slabs of smoked bacon and cut them into short lengths. When he'd weighed them on the scale, he began to call out names.

"Here, Ben, three pounds for you," Papa said to his friend.

"Jess and me's goin' fishin' after dinner if you wanta come," Ben said as he took his bacon. Sunday was the only day the slaves had free to keep their own gardens and fish to supplement the rations they got from the Master.

"I'll come on down after dinner," Titus replied. "Here you go, Rose," he said to one of Ben's little girls. "Come get your pound."

After the bacon had been handed out, they moved to the corncrib. Maddie turned down invitations for dinner at the cabins, knowing her mama would never let her go. But she told her friends Elsie and Louisa that she'd be down to visit in the afternoon. *If* she could get away from Mama, she added to herself.

"Your turn, Shad," Titus called out.

The man came to stand beside Titus. Maddie was busy scooping out his ration of corn when she heard him whisper, "We's ready. Tonight, when the moon's high."

Maddie's head jerked up. She saw the tension in her papa's face, but Shad's expression was calm. He was even smiling a little.

Titus took the corn from Maddie. He squeezed Shad's hands as the ration of corn passed between them. Shad just nodded and grinned. Then he winked at Maddie before he walked away.

After giving out the corn, Maddie and Titus headed back to the kitchen quarter in silence. Maddie's head was buzzing with questions she longed to ask Papa. But she hesitated, not sure she was ready to hear the answers.

What had Shad meant when he told Papa they were ready? It must be the plan Papa had told Mama about. But taking one of Master's rifles! Slaves weren't allowed to have weapons. Master would surely skin 'em alive if he found out.

They had to be planning to run away. Tonight, when the moon was high. And Papa knew! A hard knot of fear twisted in Maddie's belly. Papa could be in trouble, himself, just for knowing about it. Master might flog him with the bullwhip. Or worse!

Maddie reached for Titus's hand and squeezed it hard. He looked down at her with questions in his eyes.

She ignored the look, too frightened to give words to her feelings. Her heart was beating fast and hard in her chest. She didn't want Papa mixed up in Shad and Caleb's plan. She just wanted him safe! The same as Mama.

Sometimes Mama made her mad because she never wanted Papa and Maddie to do the things they enjoyed—like visiting the folks at the cabins. But maybe Mama was right this time. If there was going to be trouble at the cabins, Papa shouldn't be down there!

Maddie thought suddenly of Elsie's mama. Like Ella and Titus, Bertie had been born at River Bend. But Bertie was a field slave, and her life had always been harder. One day, when Maddie was just a little girl, Bertie had been too sick to go to the fields. She had figured Master would beat her for not working, so she'd run off and hidden in the woods. But Master hired the pattyrollers to hunt her down. There was no way Bertie could escape those men and their tracking dogs. Next day they dragged her back. She was stripped and tied to a post so Master could give her fifty lashes with his bullwhip. Aunt Lucy said that girl screamed louder than any slave she'd ever heard, till the pain got too much and she passed out.

Maddie was five or six the next time Bertie tried to run. She was in the kitchen with Mama when the men brought Bertie back. Maddie remembered the sounds of the men shouting and the hounds yelping, all excited because they'd tracked down the runaway's scent. But Mama wouldn't let Maddie go outside to see. All the while Master was flogging Bertie, Mama just kept singing "Swing Low, Sweet Chariot" real loud to cover the shrieks and wails. But it didn't help. Bertie's screams carried to every corner of the plantation.

It wasn't until days later, when Bertie was on her feet again but still a pitiful sight, that Maddie saw the Master had done more than just flog her. Bertie was passing the kitchen quarter on her way to the fields. Maddie could see the woman's face was swollen and red as blood. But the worst sight was the horrible oozing sore on her cheek. Maddie thought she was going to be sick when she saw it. The Master had *branded* Bertie with a hot iron! For the rest of her life poor Bertie would carry the shameful mark on her once-pretty face. The *R* for runaway. Bertie never did try to leave the plantation after that.

"Daughter, what's goin' on in that busy head'a yours?"

Maddie started at her papa's voice. She was shivering, even with the warm morning sun on her back. "Shad and Caleb's plannin' to run," she blurted out. "They took Master's rifle—"

"Hush!" Titus gripped her shoulder and shook her hard. Maddie was shocked by his rough treatment and by the harshness of his voice.

Titus's face softened. "Let's set a spell."

She followed him to the shade of the old walnut trees by the carriage house. Titus was silent for a while, chewing on a blade of grass while he stared thoughtfully at the Big House. When he finally spoke, his voice was grave.

"You know what'd happen if Master or Mistress heard a slave was plannin' to run off, don't you?"

"They'd whip him."

"That's right. Whether it was true or not. So we don't talk about that where somebody might hear. Understand?"

Maddie looked down at the ground. "I'm sorry, Papa. I was thinkin' about Bertie, what happened when she ran off—and I was scared for you. I don't want 'em to hurt you!"

Titus frowned, still staring at the Big House. "Don't you fret—nobody's gonna hurt your papa."

"Mama's scared they will."

Titus sighed. "Your ears are gettin' too big for the rest'a you, I reckon. Well, you just open them big ears and listen good, you hear? I respect your mama a powerful lot, but that don't mean I always think like her. She sees her family safe and fed, and she don't want no more than that. But *I* want more! Not just for me—for your mama and you children, too."

"You want to be free," Maddie said, repeating what she had heard the night before. "But what does that mean, Papa?"

"It means havin' your own plot'a land that belongs to you," Titus said slowly. "You kin work that land and sell the harvest and keep the money you make. It means bein' able to read and write without breakin' the law." His voice grew louder and bolder as he spoke. "It's knowin' you kin walk away from this place without riskin' the bullwhip if they catch you."

"But Mama don't wanta walk away."

"She's scared'a leavin' what she knows."

"And she's scared of the bluecoats," Maddie said. "Why's Mama so scared and you're not?"

" 'Cause your mama puts too much store in what Mistress tells her. She was raised in the Big House, right alongside the Mistress, so she has a special feelin' for the woman that you and me don't have. But, Maddie," he said with sudden intensity, "I hears the bluecoats don't hold with ownin' other folks, no matter what the color'a their skin. Seems to me, they thinks more of us slaves than Master and Mistress ever did."

After dinner, Angeline told Mama she was going to pick up pecans. Maddie saw her chance to get away for a while. "I'll come, too," she said. But instead of following Angeline to the pecan grove, Maddie headed straight for slave row.

The cabins were built of rough logs, with clay daubed in to keep out wind and rain. They stood close together in two rows, divided by a dusty road that turned to red mud when the rains came.

Elsie and her older sister, Delia, were sitting outside when Maddie got there. Younger children were playing a ring game nearby, their voices shrill and carefree as they sang.

> *Ole Massa likewise promise me*
> *When he died, he'd set me free,*
> *But ole Massa go an' make a will*
> *Fer to leave me a-pickin' cotton still.*

"Thought you wasn't comin'," Elsie said when Maddie sat down beside her. "Miz Ella give you trouble?"

Maddie shook her head, embarrassed that they all knew how her mama felt about her visiting the cabins. Like she thought Maddie was better than her friends. "Had to clean up after dinner."

"You comin' to the gatherin'-in?" Delia asked, not looking up from the shirt she was patching.

"If it's not too busy at the Big House."

Each autumn, after the cotton had been picked and the corn laid by, Master gave the field hands a day off and slaughtered steers for a barbecue. They danced to the music of Ben's fiddle and sang and ate far into the night. Papa always went to the gatherin'-in, but Mama usually found things for Maddie to do. It was times like that when Maddie wondered if she was really better off than Elsie and Louisa.

Elsie seemed to think so. She was forever telling Maddie how blessed she was. Why, didn't she have two sturdy workday dresses, gray in summer and dark blue in winter, and wool stockings, and even a change of petticoats? Elsie had only one flimsy homespun dress a year, always outgrown before she got a new one at Christmas. But she didn't seem to resent Maddie's good fortune. Even so, Maddie was careful to take off her shoes and white apron before coming to the cabins.

"Mama's been askin' about you," Elsie said. "Let's see her 'fore we find Louisa."

The cabin had no windows. The only light came from the open door and the fire in the small fireplace when it was lit. There was no fire today, so the little room was in deep shadow. Maddie could just make out the rough table in the center and the row of thin pallets on the dirt floor. Bertie recognized Maddie at once, however, and ran to hug her with strong arms.

"If it ain't little Maddie," she said in her low, gravelly voice. "Where you been, chile? I ain't seen you in two—no, more like three—Sundays. They keep you tied up in that Big House?"

"No, ma'am. Aunt Lucy's been poorly and I've been helpin' with Pride," Maddie said.

"Po' Aunt Lucy." Bertie clucked and shook her kerchiefed head. "Sho' do wish there was sump'n I could do to ease her pain, after all she done for me and mine."

Maddie had grown so used to the scar on Bertie's cheek, she rarely noticed it anymore. But today, even in the dim light, the big, ugly *R* seemed to leap out at her—reminding her of Shad and Caleb's plan, and of her fears for Papa.

Bertie was studying her with kind eyes. "You lookin' a mite peaked, Maddie. You be doin' all right?"

Maddie nodded, unable to bring herself to look at the woman's face again.

"And how's Ella? And Angeline and Pride?"

"Fine. Pride's so big now, Mama says she won't have a knee-baby much longer."

"Well, Miz Maddie, I knows you been missin' my ash cakes," Bertie said. "Just set yo'self down and I'll fix you one swimmin' in molasses."

"Mama, Maddie done had dinner," Elsie said quickly. "We's goin' to Louisa's."

"You don't say." Bertie grinned. "Run along then. But, Maddie, you promise you'll come back and visit with Bertie real soon, you hear? I tells yo' papa, I sez, that Maddie's a fine gal, a mighty fine gal—and always welcome here, same as one'a my own."

After another fierce hug, Maddie was free to follow Elsie out into the sunshine.

"Mama thinks the sun done rise and set on yo' papa, that's why she makes on over you like she does," Elsie said as they walked down the road toward Louisa's cabin. "Ever'body in the cabins say Titus is one fine man."

Maddie allowed the warmth of her friend's words to

wash over her like a summer rain, feeling proud enough to bust that they all loved and respected Papa as she did.

"My mama say it's Titus gonna show us the way to freedom," Elsie continued merrily, kicking at a dirt clod as she skipped along. "Last night at the meetin' yo' papa say they nothin' worth fightin' for but fam'ly and freedom. He say we gotta be willin' to fight if we wants to be free."

Maddie was stunned. Then Elsie went to the meetings too? Probably all the older children went—all but Angeline and herself. They heard her papa talk about things she knew nothing about. They probably even knew about Shad and Caleb running away.

All of a sudden Maddie realized she was mad. Mad at Mama for keeping her from the meetings. Mad at Elsie for talking about it in the first place.

"Ain't yo' proud'a yo' papa for bein' so brave?" Elsie asked, stooping to pick a morning glory from alongside the road.

"If you keep runnin' your mouth and dallyin', we'll never get to Louisa's," Maddie snapped, not knowing that she sounded just like Mama when Mama was afraid.

Four

Next morning Maddie was helping Ella and Angeline in the kitchen when Luther came in to tell them two slaves had run off.

"They wasn't nowhere to be found when it come time to go to the fields," Luther said. "Master's spittin' nails. He done sent for the pattyrollers and the dogs."

Maddie's heart was pounding so hard she figured they could see it trying to bust out of her chest. She glanced at her mama and saw that Ella's face looked pinched and ashen.

Angeline looked frightened. "Who was it ran off?" she asked.

"Shad and that no-'count Caleb." Luther scowled and spat into the fire. "I knowed that slave was trouble the minute he set foot on the place. You 'member I tell you that, Ella?"

"Where's Titus?" Ella asked weakly, ignoring his question.

"Master done sent him on to the fields," Luther said. "Sez Titus don't know nothin' about them runnin' off. They's gonna be two sorry slaves when the pattyrollers brings 'em back. Ole Shad should'a knowed better."

Maddie worked hard all day, racing from one chore to the next without waiting for Ella to remind her. She wanted to ease her mama's burden, but there was little she could do to calm Ella's fears. Or her own.

She was carrying out a pan of dishwater to empty in the kitchen yard when the Master came riding in that afternoon. He was going at such a gallop, he left great clouds of dust in his wake. Maddie could see he was in a temper, the way he whipped the poor sweating horse with his crop and snarled at the stable boy.

She hurried to get out of his way, but she was not quick enough. He brushed against her as he strode toward the house, upsetting the pan in her arms. Greasy water sloshed all over, drenching the front of her dress as well as his fine boots and britches.

"Clumsy little fool!" Master looked up from his soiled trousers to Maddie's frightened face. His blue eyes were dark with rage. "What you doin' here? Why aren't you in the fields?"

"I—I help my mama in the kitchen," Maddie stammered. "And with the housework. I sweep and dust—"

"What's your mama called?"

"Ella, Master."

"Well, you tell Ella her girl won't be needed in the house no more," the Master said in a cold voice. "You're to go to the fields in the mornin'."

"Yes, Master," Maddie mumbled.

She watched miserably as he stalked across the yard into the house. That was how Ella found her a while later.

"What you standin' there for?" Ella demanded. "With all the work there is, we don't have time for no woolgatherin'." Her eyes fell on Maddie's wet dress. "You spill that dishwater?"

27

"Master ran into me—"

"Lord be patient," Ella muttered. "You get Master wet?"

Maddie nodded, fighting back tears.

"And him mad as the devil to begin with," Ella said. "What did he say?"

"Told me to go to the fields in the mornin'."

"Sweet Jesus," Ella whispered. She grabbed the pan from Maddie. "You go on home and change outta that wet dress. Help Aunt Lucy with Pride the rest'a the day."

Maddie didn't move. "I didn't mean to spill the water, Mama."

"I know." Ella glanced at the house, her face unreadable. "You don't worry, Maddie. Master's in such a tizzy he won't even 'member what he said tomorrow. You just stay outta that man's way, you hear? Go on with you now."

That night Titus came in later than usual. Ella met him at the door.

He patted her arm and sat down wearily. Maddie came to sit at his feet and lay her head against his knees.

"Thought we would never finish," Titus said. "The workers was too jumpy to care about pickin'—kept watchin' the road to see if the pattyrollers was comin' back."

"You told Master you didn't know about no runaways?" Ella demanded.

"I told him."

"And he believed you?"

Titus stroked Maddie's hair. "Seemed to."

"They got the dogs out, Titus. You know they'll never get away."

Maddie felt her papa's hand tense up, then relax. "We

kin hope, Ella. And say a prayer for 'em—eh, Maddie girl?"

Next day Ella kept Maddie in the kitchen with her, rolling out dough for pies and biscuits, and washing up after the cooking. Angeline took care of the dusting and sweeping.

Every time the kitchen door opened, Maddie cringed, expecting to see the Master fly in to drag her out to the fields. She was ashamed now of ever thinking she'd want to change places with Elsie.

Nancy came to the kitchen in the afternoon to fix the Mistress some tea. Maddie could tell she was fairly bursting to tell them something.

"You look like you done set in a hill'a ants," Luther remarked. "Cain't hardly stay still, kin you, Nancy?"

The woman grinned. "Don't pretend you not dyin' to know what's happenin', ole man. 'Course, if you ain't curious about Shad and Caleb—"

"What you know about them?" Ella cut in.

"Oh, just what I heared Master tell Mistress," Nancy said. "Ella, this tea don't seem nearly hot enough to suit Mistress."

"Nancy, quit your foolin' and tell us what you know," Ella said.

"Just that Master tole Mistress one of 'em's been caught."

"Which one?" Luther wanted to know.

"Master didn't say. Reckon he don't much care." Nancy was frowning now, all her sassiness gone. "He was clear in the next county, hidin' in a corncrib. The dogs got him, Master say, plumb tore him up. The pattyrollers is bringin' him back now."

"Lord have mercy," Luther muttered.

They watched through the kitchen door as the pattyrollers brought in their captive. First came three white men on horseback and a pack of barking hounds. Slung over the back of a fourth horse was the motionless body of a man Maddie recognized.

She couldn't see his face, but she knew by the old red bandanna around his neck that it was Shad. His shirt and trousers were torn where the dogs had gotten to him, and were soaked in blood.

Angeline made a little noise, like the whimper of a puppy. The rest of them were silent.

Maddie saw Master walk across the yard, the leather bullwhip in his hand. Surely he wouldn't whip a man who was already more dead than alive, Maddie thought. She looked frantically to her mama, not knowing what any of them could do, but feeling they had to do something. Ella just stared into the yard.

Master grabbed Shad by the hair and pulled his head up. Maddie could see the slave's mouth was hanging open, his eyes closed. He looked dead already. And maybe that would be a blessing, she thought—at least he'd be past the point where the Master could hurt him.

She thought about the last time she'd seen Shad. How he'd grinned at Papa and winked at her. The scene in the kitchen yard blurred, and she turned away.

Shad didn't die from the hounds' mauling. Since he was out cold when the pattyrollers brought him in, Master didn't flog him either. But he was tied like a dog to a post in the kitchen yard and left to heal on his own. Once a day Shad's wife was permitted to bring him water. The other slaves were warned not to go near him. And nobody did.

For a week Shad crouched or lay in the yard, the ropes

that bound his hands to the post too short to allow him to stand up. When the rains came hard for two days without letting up, it was all Maddie could do to keep from running out to the kitchen yard to cut those ropes. But even Papa didn't seem to understand. He said he'd whip her good, himself, if she went anywhere near Shad.

Finally, the Master untied him. Leaning on his wife, Shad hobbled painfully to their cabin. A few days later he was back in the fields. But Maddie noticed that he never smiled after that. And when she passed him and spoke, he kept his eyes to the ground and acted like he hadn't heard.

Five

A utumn went by slowly for Maddie. Even though Mistress was up and running the house again, she passed on her silent melancholy to the servants, and there was little talk or merriment to break up the long, tedious days. And the Master seemed to stay angry. He had placed notices in papers as far away as Savannah, Georgia, and Richmond, Virginia, offering a five-hundred-dollar reward for the return of his property, "a well set Negro named Caleb." But Caleb seemed to have vanished from the earth. And the longer he was gone, the more irate the Master became. Maddie made sure she stayed out of his way.

She was in trouble with Mama more often than usual now. There were times when she thought she couldn't stand the gloom of the Big House another minute and fell back into the habit of disappearing when nobody was looking.

In some ways, the nights in the kitchen quarter were worse than the days. The tension between Mama and Papa never eased up. Maddie found herself watching them all the time, hoping to see a sign of their old affection for each other. But they acted like strangers, their voices cool and distant. Mama didn't hum anymore as she worked, and Papa never smiled or teased Maddie. Even

Angeline, who never worried about anything, followed them with soft, puzzled eyes.

The only good change Maddie could see was that Mistress no longer seemed to care whether Maddie was insolent or not. Mistress swept through the house, barely noticing Maddie and the others at all. She would tell Ella what she wanted for meals the next day, but she left most everything else to Ella and Luther. Even Nancy was baffled by her mistress's behavior.

"You know how fussy she always was about her hair," Nancy was saying in the kitchen one day. "Now she cain't set still long enough for me to fix it. When I'm half done, she just gits up and wanders off with most'a it trailin' down her back. And she's real skittish. If I walks up behind her and she don't know I'm there, she shrieks like I come to murder her."

"It's a hard thing to lose a child," Ella said softly, and Maddie knew she was thinking about her own dead sons. "We gotta be patient."

Nancy shrugged. "She kin grieve the rest'a her life, for all I care. She's a whole lot less trouble to me this way."

Ella gave her a hard look and Nancy grinned. "Anyhow, I think it's more'n young Master Jamie preyin' on her mind these days. I heared her talkin' to the Master last night about the Yankee soldiers, and she's mighty afeared of 'em. Sez she don't plan to just set and wait for them devils to show up one day and kill us all."

"It's not your place to spread talk 'tween the Master and the Mistress," Ella chided her.

"Master don't think the bluecoats'll ever make it this far," Nancy went on, as though Ella hadn't spoken. "Lot

33

he knows! Bet they's here 'fore Christmas. And won't we have somethin' to celebrate then!"

Maddie felt a twinge of excitement when she heard Nancy's words. If the woman was right, they could be free before the new year began. But if they didn't stay at River Bend, where would they go? Were there cotton plantations in the North for them to work? If Master and Mistress weren't in charge, who would be? Maddie had a hard time imagining what freedom would be like.

Several days later, she overheard a conversation that only added to her confusion. The Mistress was entertaining her mother, who lived on a nearby plantation, and a few of her closest lady friends. Ella had prepared a tray of cakes for Maddie to carry into the parlor.

"And mind you don't drop the tray," Ella warned her, as she handed it to Maddie. "Just set it on the table by Mistress, wait to see if she needs anything else, curtsy, and leave. Understand?"

"Yes, Mama."

The tray was heavy, but Maddie managed to carry it to the parlor and place it on the table without embarrassing either herself or Ella. Then she stood back to wait, as Ella had directed. Only nobody noticed that she was there. They just went on talking without giving her a thought.

"Althea, you're a fool if you believe our boys can keep those savages out of North Carolina," the old Mistress said, shaking her silver head. The rustling of her taffeta dress emphasized her agitation. "The Confederacy has youth and valor on its side, but we don't have the weapons they have."

"Mother, you're talkin' treason." The Mistress was obviously upset, her pretty face appearing paler than usual against the black of her mourning clothes. "You know the South'll win the war. Everybody says so."

"'Course the Confederacy will win," one of the other ladies agreed, frowning at the old Mistress. "My Thomas says we'll be rid of those brutes 'fore summer."

"And last summer your Thomas said we'd beat 'em in three weeks," the old woman reminded her. "Listen to me, children, the Yankees won't let North Carolina escape untouched."

"But why should they want to change our way of life?" the Mistress demanded. "Don't they see that our way is best for everybody? We mind our own business, work our land, and take care of our people. Why do those spiteful Yankees want to ruin everythin'?"

"They're jealous, that's what," said another of the Mistress's friends. "I've been to the North and I can tell you, there's absolutely no grace or charm anywhere up there. And the servants! They do exactly as they please. They're allowed to talk back—it's deplorable! When the Yankees see our people so well behaved and *wantin'* to serve us—*lovin'* us for what we do for them—they must turn green with envy."

"I've always tried to do my best by our people," the Mistress said absently. She looked up and stared straight into Maddie's dark eyes. "What are you doin' lurkin' around?" she snapped. "We won't be needin' anythin' else," she added in a cold voice.

"Hard to believe that's my Ella's girl." Maddie heard this as she turned to leave. "Never have trusted that surly little wench—the way she sneaks around and listens to everythin' we say."

It wasn't until Maddie reached the kitchen that she realized she had forgotten to curtsy.

35

"We won't need you in the kitchen no more today," Ella told her when she saw Maddie. "Go help Aunt Lucy with Pride. And take in the wash on your way."

Maddie was more than happy to escape from the Big House, if only for the afternoon. The Mistress's reference to Ella's "surly little wench" had made her feel small and ashamed. She had only been trying to do what her mama told her. She hadn't meant to overhear the ladies' talk. It seemed that there was no way to please the Mistress. And Maddie realized suddenly that way down inside she wasn't even sure she wanted to.

Aunt Lucy was stirring a pot over the fire when Maddie came in with the stack of folded sheets.

"Come help me, girl. My arm's plumb give out."

Maddie took the wooden spoon and stared at the yellowish liquid in the pot. Bits of leaves floated in it. "What is this, Aunt Lucy?" she asked, hoping the woman wouldn't tell her it was something for supper.

"A brew for young Lettie." Aunt Lucy sank down into a rocker. "Her youngun's due most any day. This'll ease the pain some."

Maddie wrinkled her nose at the strong smell of the brew. "What are these leaves?"

"Raspberry. I give 'em to Ella when Pride was comin'. Was the easiest birthin' I ever did see. I should'a been teachin' you more," Aunt Lucy went on. "You're the only one with a feel for doctorin'. But it's near too late now."

Maddie looked up. "What you mean, too late?"

"I'm an ole woman, chile. Already lived past my time." Her voice was matter-of-fact. "By the time my granny's end was near, she could rest easy, knowin' she'd passed on to me all *her* granny had learned her. Don't have no

36

gran'chillun of my own, but I thinks of you that way. It would'a been fittin' to hand down what I knows to you."

"There's plenty'a time to teach me," Maddie said sharply, defying her to argue. She had heard enough lately about life changing. She had no intention of losing Aunt Lucy along with everything else.

Six

It was the day before Christmas, and Maddie had never seen such a flurry of activity as was going on in the Big House. Luther had overseen the men bringing the huge evergreen tree into the front hall, where it now stood in a tub waiting to be trimmed. Maddie and Angeline had spent days making garlands of running cedar to be tied with red ribbons along the stair railings and over the doors. They had made centerpieces from fruit and holly and evergreen boughs until their fingers ached. And they still had baking to do and cleaning to finish.

Since the Master and Mistress were still in mourning, it was understood that there would be no parties for their neighbors this year, but the Mistress had insisted on decorating the house as usual. Luther told Maddie that young Master Jamie had loved Christmas better than anything, and his mama couldn't bear not having a tree for him. Only the black bows on the door and the Master's and Mistress's somber mourning clothes reminded everybody that neither of the young Masters would be there to celebrate this year.

After their day's work in the Big House was done, Ella, Angeline, and Maddie went back to their quarters to fix supper and work on their own Christmas celebration. Angeline had been gathering nuts, berries, and apples for months to put in the pies and cakes they would bake.

The weather had been unusually warm for December, but the week before Christmas a cold snap had hit. There was even talk of snow. Snow in December meant a good crop for the year ahead, according to the old slaves, who reminisced about Christmas barbecues long ago with a layer of the white stuff on the ground.

Maddie watched the gray sky hopefully. She hadn't seen a great many snows in her life, but it didn't take much to make the plantation breathtakingly beautiful. And if the ponds froze, she and Elsie and Louisa could slide across the ice and fall into soft snowdrifts on the other side.

After supper, the family took turns bathing in the wash-tub and then dressed in their Sunday best. Maddie could hardly breathe in the high-necked brown dress that was nearly a year old and was now way too tight and short. But she knew better than to complain. Mama was going to make sure that her family looked its best when they went to the Big House for Christmas.

When it was time, they walked to the house and waited in the kitchen until Luther came to get them. He made a big fuss over them before leading them into the receiving hall, complimenting Maddie's dress and telling Angeline she was nearly as pretty as her mama had been at her age.

Maddie was just plain scared of seeing the Master face-to-face again—or of *him* seeing *her*—after his fury over the spilled dishwater. But when she walked into the hall and saw the tree, her fears were forgotten. The beauty of the glistening evergreen always filled her with awe. She longed to step closer and touch it. But one look from Mama and she restrained the urge.

The Master and Mistress were standing by the staircase, smiling at them. Maddie thought Mistress looked truly beautiful, even in the black mourning dress, her golden hair gleaming in the candlelight like an angel's. And the Master looked kind as he picked up the heavy Bible and began to read the story of Jesus's birth.

Maddie had always liked the story of the poor little baby born in a stable. She especially liked the part about everybody traveling for miles and miles to bring gifts to the child. But she noticed as the reading went on that Nancy was fidgeting and Luther was nearly asleep. Papa had a tight look on his face, as though angered by being invited to the Big House for Christmas. Only Mama and Angeline seemed to enjoy the story, their eyes bright as they took in the sights around them.

After a while, even Maddie grew tired from standing so long. She was glad when Master finally closed the Bible and began to tell them what good jobs they had done that year. Then Mistress echoed his words, with especially warm smiles for Mama and Angeline, Maddie thought, and the Master began to pass out gifts.

There was whiskey for Luther and Papa, though more for Luther, since he was a house servant. And a new shirt and pants for Papa. Mama received bolts of gray and dark blue cloth to make work dresses for Angeline, Maddie, and herself, and three pieces of fabric for their good dresses. Maddie always hoped that one year she'd have a red dress, but the cloth was dark green, dark gray, and brown. Luther got his new uniform and Nancy cloth for her dresses, and all of them were given their annual pair of shoes. As always, Maddie's shoes were too big and so stiff the leather would cut into tender feet like an ax blade. But after Mama rubbed them with tallow a few times, they would be as soft as Mistress's slippers.

"But wait, now, that's not all," the Master said gleefully. And digging into a burlap sack, he withdrew a crushed felt hat, which he gave to Papa, a gray shawl for Mama, and mittens for the three children. It was obvious that the mittens had been worn by others for a very long time; there were even holes in the thumbs of Maddie's. But she was overjoyed when she saw them. Now she could make snowballs without freezing her hands. And best of all, the mittens were *red!*

Master was watching them with a benign smile. How different he looked tonight from the angry man with the bullwhip. "Go back to your quarters and fall to your knees," he told them. "Praise the good Lord for bein' blessed with a lovin' Master and Mistress. Thank Him for seein' fit to put you in our care. And remember that an offense against your Master and Mistress is an offense against God, Himself. So be faithful, be humble, and bear your burdens with joy and gratitude. And Titus, you take tomorrow off and enjoy the barbecue with your family."

For a moment no one spoke. Then Ella said in a fluttery voice, "Thank you, Master. How good you and Mistress are to us."

The Master smiled at Ella and patted her cheek. Then Luther led them away to the kitchen.

It wasn't until they were back in the kitchen quarter that Maddie realized Mama was mad. Not just annoyed or fretful, but *mad!* She threw the bolts of cloth on the table and turned to her husband with fury in her eyes.

"Not now, Ella," he said wearily. "Not on the eve of Christmas."

"Would it of been too much to say, 'Thank you, Master'?' After all he gave us, would one little 'thank you' have been too hard?"

"After all *he* gave *us?*" Titus laughed, but the sound was bitter. "What about what *we* give *him?* He wouldn't have a roof over his head or a horse under his saddle if it wasn't for us. You 'spect me to be grateful for a suit'a clothes and torn mittens for my children? Well, I cain't be, wife." He tossed the clothes and hat to the floor and glared at her. "I cain't believe you'd ask it of me."

Then he was gone, slamming the door behind him.

Seven

Maddie had reason to be grateful for the hand-me-down mittens when the temperatures dropped even lower after Christmas. She came to dread the mornings because it was her job to draw icy water from the well and to gather eggs from the henhouse. She envied Mama and Angeline their work in the warm kitchen.

Now that the cotton was picked and the corn laid by, Titus didn't have to go to the fields again until plowing time in the spring. But he put in long days, just the same, cutting wood, mending fences, and repairing outbuildings with the other field slaves. It was still way after dark when he came home for supper.

Maddie usually ran outside to meet him. She would know the workers were coming in when she heard the singing of a Sorrow Song—the only kind of song they knew. Sometimes she and Papa would walk with the others as far as the cabins, their voices raised with the rest.

Go 'way, Ole Man,
Go 'way, Ole Man,
Where you been all day?
If you treats me good
I'll stay 'til Judgment Day,
But if you treats me bad,
I'm sho' to run away.

Since before Christmas, Maddie had had a case of what Ella called "the jitters." She felt jumpy all the time, like she was waiting for something bad to happen. She kept watching her mama and papa, hoping for a sign that they were getting on better, and she found herself listening for any mention of the war. It was all tied together— Mama and Papa's trouble, Maddie's restlessness, and the approach of the Yankees. Maddie wished the bluecoats would just come on, whether they were going to kill them all or set them free. Anything was better than the waiting!

In that, at least, Maddie and the Mistress had something in common. After Christmas was over, Mistress McCartha had more time to dwell on her fears of the Yankees, and she was even more impatient with the house staff than usual. Finally, one day, she screamed at Angeline for putting too much starch in her petticoats and ran sobbing from the kitchen.

Ella, Angeline, and Maddie stared after her in disbelief. None of them had ever seen the Mistress cry, not even after young Master Jamie died. But even more incredible to Maddie was the fact that Mistress had raised her voice to Angeline.

It was two days later when Nancy came to the kitchen looking smug and told Ella that Mistress wanted to see her in the parlor.

Ella wiped her hands hurriedly on her apron and turned questioning eyes to Nancy. "What does she want?"

" 'Spect you'll find out quick enough," Nancy said sassily, " 'less you stand here all day tryin' to figger it out."

"Someday that mouth'a yours is gonna open once too often," Ella muttered.

She was gone a long time. When she came back, her face revealed nothing.

"What did Mistress want, Mama?" Angeline asked anxiously when Ella made no move to speak.

"She told me we're goin' away."

"The bluecoats are here," Maddie whispered, not realizing she had spoken until Ella turned to her.

"Not yet, girl, but Mistress fears they will be any day. Master says she'll be safer at the summer house."

For as long as Maddie could remember, the Mistress had left the plantation in July to join her sister and her mother at the summer house at Nags Head. Maddie wasn't sure just where Nags Head was, but she knew it was far away. She had heard the young Masters talk about taking a ship to get there and bathing in the ocean with their friends.

But this year the Mistress hadn't gone to the summer house. Everybody had expected the war to be over in a few weeks, and many had delayed their holidays to wait for loved ones to return from the army. Now, of course, young Master Jamie wouldn't be coming home at all, and nobody knew when to expect young Master Andrew.

"And we're goin' with her?" Angeline clapped her hands together. "Did you hear that, Maddie? We're goin' to the ocean."

"Don't be too joyful about it," Nancy grumbled. "She'll keep you workin' there same as here. And the worst part is we'll be gone when the bluecoats comes to set us free."

"Or shoot us," Ella snapped.

"Is Mistress takin' me, too?" Maddie asked softly. She could understand Mistress wanting her personal maid, and Ella to do the cooking, and even Angeline, who was always helpful. But why would she want Maddie?

" 'Course she's takin' you." Ella's voice was unusually gentle as she looked at her younger daughter. "I told the Mistress I wouldn't be much use to her if I was worryin' about my babies while I was gone."

"What about Papa?"

"Master says Mistress should have your papa along to care for the animals and get provisions."

"When we leavin'?" Angeline asked.

"Soon's Mistress can get ready," Ella replied. "A few days, I 'spect. So don't be takin' off your apron just yet, daughter. We got work to do 'tween now and then."

Ella and Angeline were kept running helping Nancy ready the Mistress for the trip, as well as doing their usual work. Maddie found herself in charge of washing and packing her own family's clothes. She didn't mind the extra work because the prospect of a journey—her first trip ever away from the plantation—was more exciting than anything that had ever happened to her.

Ella was more tolerant than usual of her younger daughter's high spirits and moments of forgetfulness. Maddie suspected that even Mama was excited about going away, not to mention feeling easier about not being there when the bluecoats came. Papa's feelings were another matter.

"What good will I be to her?" Titus had demanded when Ella told him.

"Women need a man for protection."

"A slave man, not even allowed to carry a weapon?" Titus scoffed, black eyes flashing. "A lot'a help I'll be."

"You just don't want'a miss whatever trouble you're hopin' for here at River Bend," Ella accused him.

"You're right about that," Titus agreed. "But you seem bound to save me from it."

"And someday you'll thank me for it," Ella said softly to his retreating back.

By the second week of January, they were ready to leave for Nags Head. On the morning of their departure, a grim-faced Titus carried their few bundles of clothing and bedding to the wagon that waited in front of the Big House. Ella and Angeline said their good-byes to Aunt Lucy and followed Titus with young Pride in tow. But Maddie hung back, realizing suddenly that in all the excitement of preparing to leave, she had forgotten how much she would miss Aunt Lucy.

"We won't be gone long," Maddie assured her, and came to sit at the old woman's feet. "Mistress says the Yankees'll be whipped by spring, and then we'll come back."

Aunt Lucy just smiled at Maddie and patted the girl's shoulder.

"Will you be all right by yourself?"

"Ole Lucy'll do just fine, don't you fret none. But I'll sho' be lonesome without you."

Maddie could hear Angeline calling her, but she made no move to leave. She buried her face against the old woman's knee and breathed in the pungent smell of herbs that clung to her skirts.

"They's waitin' for you," Aunt Lucy said. "But 'fore you go, I got sump'n for you. No time to open it now."

Maddie took the blue knotted kerchief with questioning eyes.

"Just some hazel root and tansy, things you might be needin'. You knows how to use 'em well enough now."

The woman patted Maddie's shoulder again and then gave her a gentle shove. "Best you be goin', girl, 'fore yo' mama take a hickory switch to you."

Maddie got slowly to her feet. Then, impulsively, she leaned down to embrace the woman. "I'll miss you, too, Aunt Lucy. But I'll be back."

"Ain't meant for ole Lucy to see you no more in this life, chile." She shook her head impatiently at Maddie's denial. "You listen to me, Maddie. It won't always be easy, but you'll come through, 'cause you got backbone. But you gotta take care of Angeline and Pride and your mama. They's not strong as you. You hear me, girl?" she demanded, her old eyes burning into Maddie's face. "You watch over 'em and do for 'em. They needs you."

"I will," Maddie promised, blinking back the tears that filled her eyes.

"Now, git on with you."

Maddie walked slowly to the door of the kitchen quarter, clutching the bundle of herbs. She stopped once to look back at the old woman, who had already turned away to stare into the fire.

PART TWO

Nags Head

JANUARY–FEBRUARY 1862

Eight

Gale-force winds, bringing with them a numbing winter rain, swept through Elizabeth City as the schooner pulled away from the dock. The vessel pitched and rolled so violently in the choppy waters of the Pasquotank River its passengers feared they would never reach Nags Head alive.

Mistress and Nancy, and even Ella, were soon feeling nauseous from the incessant rocking of the ship. Then Angeline became queasy, and finally Pride. If Titus felt ill, he kept it to himself. But Maddie had never felt better in her life! The excitement of the day was nearly too much for her to bear. She found it impossible to sit quietly as Mama demanded. After a long time of watching her twitch and squirm, Titus smiled at her—his first smile in the seven days of their journey—and told her to cover her head with her shawl; they were going out on deck.

Standing at the rail with the freezing rain blowing in her face, Maddie was the first to hear the command to drop anchor. Through the mist, she could see the darkness of forests and the vague outline of houses on a shore some half-mile away.

Soon Mistress and the other women came out on deck, faces drawn, arms laden with satchels and baskets and little Pride. The transfer of baggage and bodies to small boats that would take them on to Nags Head was a slow process, made slower by Mistress's refusal to ride in the same boat with the livestock. Maddie found herself sharing a boat with the hens, cow, and horse they had brought with them. But she preferred the odors of the animals to the ill-tempered complaints of the Mistress.

Soldiers waited for them at the dock, young, watchful men in gray uniforms who opened each bag or parcel and searched for weapons. All around them, Maddie could see mountains of wet sand, some rising bare to the winter sky, others capped with dark foliage and small white cottages. And nestled like a laying hen between two sand hills was a long, three-story building with a sign that read: NAGS HEAD HOTEL.

An older man introduced himself to Mistress as Sergeant Jakes.

"Hope you weren't plannin' on stayin' at the hotel, ma'am," he said politely but firmly. "General Wise of the Confederate Army's taken it as his headquarters."

"No, Sergeant, I have no need of the hotel," Mistress replied, sounding very much in command despite her pallor and obvious weariness. "I have a cottage here."

"Well, ma'am, it's not the best time to be at Nags Head. 'Cept for the army, and the few farmers livin' hereabouts, it's near deserted."

"I didn't come to socialize," Mistress snapped. "I'm here to protect myself from those Yankee devils."

"Yes, ma'am." The sergeant shifted uncomfortably. "We can't guarantee they won't be comin' to Nags Head, you understand. Not that we expect them to," he added hastily. "They captured Hatteras Inlet last fall, but that's not so close. We still have Nags Head and Roanoke Island."

"I should be safe enough with our soldiers here," Mistress replied, but Maddie could hear uncertainty in her voice.

"We'll take care of you and your people," Sergeant Jakes assured her. "Those Yankees just got lucky at Hatteras. But won't you be lonesome with no other white ladies for company?"

"I'll manage," Mistress said impatiently. "Can your men help my servants take the bags and animals to my house?"

The cottage was a simple two-story structure with white shingles in need of a coat of paint. It stood atop a sand hill, surrounded by a thick growth of stunted live oak and pine. On the side that overlooked the fresh water of Currituck Sound was a porch with built-in benches. On the other side was a wall of windows, now covered by wooden shutters.

"You looks out them windows, you kin sees the ocean," Nancy told Maddie as they climbed the steps to the porch.

"Nancy, stop your chatter and help get these bags inside," Mistress ordered, and Nancy scurried after her.

The cottage was not nearly so fine as the Big House at River Bend, but Maddie liked it better. It was cozier than the plantation house, with only three bedrooms upstairs, where the Mistress and Nancy would sleep, and the parlors and dining room downstairs. In a wing off the back were the kitchen and a room for Maddie and her family.

After she had helped unpack the provisions and put them away in the pantry, Maddie made their beds while Ella and Angeline cooked supper. None of them actually had beds here, just lumpy mattresses spread out on the floor. There was one scarred bureau, a straight-backed chair, and a shuttered window that Maddie looked at longingly. She could hardly wait to see what an ocean looked like.

Maddie was up first next morning. She had the fire burning in the kitchen when Ella and Titus came in.

"Good to see you makin' up for yesterday," Ella told her. "You were no help at all with us sick."

"Let up on the girl," Titus said as he pulled on his jacket. "Now you got your way about us comin' here, you can afford to be kinder."

Ella opened her mouth to speak and then shut it quickly, but Maddie saw the stern set of her mouth as she turned away to start breakfast.

"Lord only knows what I'll do to pass the days," Titus grumbled as he made for the back door. "Guess I'll go out and take a look around."

"Shouldn't I go and find the well?" Maddie asked quickly.

"Go on," Ella said, not bothering to look Maddie's way. "Take that bucket on the table."

During the night the rain had ended. The dark sky was washed with streaks of pale gold and pink as the sun began to rise. Maddie and Titus stood side by side behind the cottage, looking out over the sand dunes at the distant black waters of the Atlantic. The wind rushed and whipped at them.

Maddie breathed in the sharp odor of salt water, delighted by the sights and sounds of the place. She had never seen such a great expanse of water, nor heard anything like the roar of the waves as they crashed against the shore.

Titus noticed the rapt expression on her face. "So you like the ocean, do you, daughter?"

"Oh, yes," Maddie said. "It's so—big!"

Titus chuckled. Then Maddie heard him sigh, and she looked up, trying to gauge his mood.

He was looking at the water, his eyes moving restlessly across the distant horizon. Maddie squinted against the rising sun, scanning the line where sky and water met, but she could see nothing that might hold his attention.

"I was just thinkin' on the first time I seen this ocean," Titus said after a while. "I was a young man then. Worked on the cottage 'fore Mistress come for the summer."

"Was Mama here with you?"

"No, that was 'fore your mama and me was together." A sudden smile erased the years from his face. "Never thought your mama'd even look at me back then. She was a house servant, raised in the Big House, so she talked like them and carried herself just so. Why would she want'a take up with a field hand?"

"But you brought her flowers, anyhow," Maddie said, dredging up from memory the story Ella had told in a rare moment of nostalgia.

"Blue innocents I picked comin' in from the fields. Left 'em ever' day on the kitchen step. When the innocents was gone, I picked somethin' else, till winter come and there was no flowers left to pick."

"Then what did you do?" Maddie prompted, relishing this glimpse into her papa's past.

"Picked nuts or holly, whatever I thought she'd like."

"Did she know it was you?"

"Oh, I made sure she'd see me," he said with a grin. "Took nigh on to a year, but one evenin' she was waitin' for me when I stopped by. She said, 'They call you Titus, that right?' And I said, 'That's right.' And she said, 'Why you keep leavin' these things for me?' And I said, ' 'Cause you're the purtiest girl I ever did see.' And she said, 'You shouldn't be doin' this, it's not right.' And I said, 'If you say you'll marry me, it'll be right.' And at the next Christmas marryin', we jumped the broom."

Since the law did not allow slaves to marry, couples would jump over a broom together and declare themselves husband and wife. Maddie had been to the Christmas marryings, but it had never occurred to her that Mama and Papa had once been as shy and glowing as those young couples were.

"Tell me more, Papa," she pleaded. "What was Mama like back then?"

"Don't have time for no more stories. Your mama's waitin' for that water.'" Titus thrust his hands into his pockets and turned back to look at the ocean.

He was lost in his own thoughts again, the closeness they had shared forgotten. Gulping back her disappointment, Maddie said, "But you were talkin' about the first time you saw the ocean."

"I used to watch the ships comin' in and thought I might like to jump on one of 'em and sail away. That's all."

"Why didn't you?"

Titus shrugged. "Left for the plantation before I had a chance. Always thought I'd do it if I ever got back here."

"Did you come back?"

"Not till now."

Maddie's heart began to race. "Papa, does that mean—?"

"No, girl," he said sharply, before she could finish. "Just

a boy's dream I was tellin' you, long dead and buried. I'd never leave your mama and you children. Now, fill that bucket and go help your mama."

There was no well, so Maddie made several trips a day to the freshwater ponds scattered throughout the woods. She liked going for water because it gave her a chance to look around.

There were other cottages nestled in the woodlands, all of them shuttered and empty now, and two small farms that were lived in year-round. One day Maddie saw a young black man grooming a horse at one of the farms. She hurried back to tell Ella and Angeline.

"That's Harley Tate's place," Nancy informed them. "He's just one step above po' white trash, only got the one slave."

"Don't seem to be many slave owners in these parts," Titus remarked.

"Naw, these folks is too po'," Nancy said with a touch of arrogance.

Maddie saw soldiers wherever she went, all of them in gray uniforms like the soldiers who had met them at the dock. Mostly they ignored her when she passed them in the woods, but she could feel their eyes following her as she made her way back to the cottage. Like they wanted to make sure she wasn't trying to run away.

Life was easier here than back at the plantation. Nancy took care of Mistress's personal needs, so Ella, Angeline, and Maddie had only to cook the meals and do the washing and cleaning. Titus made several trips a week in Mistress's two-wheeled cart to pick up meat from the local farmers, and he cared for the animals they had brought. When that was done, his time was his own. Most afternoons, he'd go off by himself and come back around suppertime. Sometimes he brought a string of fish he'd caught in one of the ponds.

Ella was happier. Maddie could feel her mama begin to unwind, so the rest of them were able to relax too. They laughed more, and Ella often hummed as she worked. Only Titus remained somber. And watchful, Maddie thought, wondering what he was watching for.

Nine

Maddie was beating rugs on the porch one afternoon when Titus came back from fishing. He wasn't alone.

"Daughter, this here's Royall. Think you already spied on him over at Mister Tate's place." Titus grinned at her. "Royall, this here's my girl Maddie."

"Pleased to meetcha, Miz Maddie," the young man said softly.

He was very tall. And so good-looking, Maddie felt suddenly shy.

"Come on, Royall, and meet the rest'a the family," Titus said.

Maddie watched them disappear around the corner of the house. She threw down her broom and raced after them.

Ella seemed to like Royall at once, which wasn't usually her way. She was cautious about strangers. Maddie watched in wonder as her mama pulled up a stool for the young man and told Angeline to fetch him something to drink.

"Workin' the Tate place by yourself must be hard," Ella said. She placed a slice of her apple pie in front of him.

"Not so hard," Royall said. He cut into the pie.

"They's only thirty acres. Ummm, Miz Ella, this is the best pie I ever tasted."

"Angeline made a berry cobbler for supper." Ella looked at Angeline, who was standing strangely silent beside Maddie, her eyes on her feet. "You're welcome to stay, Royall."

"That's mighty kind'a you, Miz Ella." Royall, too, glanced at Angeline. "If you're sure it's no trouble for you and your daughters."

"It's no trouble," Angeline said before Ella could answer. Her voice sounded peculiar to Maddie, high and breathless.

Maddie watched as Angeline and Royall smiled at each other and then ducked their heads. She wasn't sure what was going on. But whatever it was, it seemed to make Ella happy, the way she was smiling at everybody and actually stopping her work to visit with a stranger!

Royall started coming over for supper nearly every night. After the meal, they would gather around the fire in the kitchen and talk. Then Royall and Angeline started going outside to sit, and Maddie finally understood what was happening. Angeline and Royall were courting.

Royall had more freedom than any slave Maddie had ever seen. "All Mister Tate cares about is gettin' the work done," he told them. "After I'm through for the day, I kin go fishin' or take my boat to Roanoke Island—whatever I feels like doin'."

"Does he whip you?" Maddie asked.

"Daughter," Ella said sharply.

Royall laughed and pulled at one of Maddie's braids. "I guess he might if I didn't do my work."

Maddie liked Royall well enough, but she had some trouble thinking about her sister with a beau. Even though Angeline would be fourteen that summer, she didn't seem that much older than Maddie. And Maddie couldn't picture herself courting for years and years.

Maybe because he sensed that Maddie had not accepted him, Royall spent extra time with her in the evenings. Sometimes he even came over in the afternoons to take her into the hills to fish. And Ella always let her go.

It had never entered Maddie's head that Angeline and Royall might not be allowed to stay together, until one night when Maddie heard her mama and papa talking.

The children were in bed, but Ella and Titus were still sitting by the fire. Unable to sleep, Maddie slid off the mattress she shared with Angeline and Pride, and opened the door to the kitchen. The impatience in her papa's voice caused her to stop and listen.

"With the war goin' on and Master needin' money, he's not gonna buy more slaves," Titus was saying.

"Well, we gotta do somethin'," Ella said. "If Angeline has to go back to River Bend without Royall, her heart's gonna break."

"Why'd you push the two of 'em together, knowin' they'd most likely have to leave each other?"

"You're the one brought him here in the first place," Ella snapped. Then she said, "I'm gonna ask Mistress if she'll talk to Master about buyin' Royall. He's strong and healthy. He'd work hard for 'em."

"What if Mister Tate don't wanta sell?" Titus asked. " 'Sides which, ain't Angeline a mite young for you to be pairin' her off?"

At least Papa saw that Angeline was too young for all this courting foolishness, Maddie thought as she crept back to bed. What had come over Mama, anyhow?

The next day an icy rain fell on Nags Head. Maddie

shivered as she carried water back from the pond. When she opened the door to the kitchen, she heard an anguished wail from inside.

Angeline was sitting at the table, her face hidden in her apron, shoulders shaking with sobs. Ella was telling her to hush up before Mistress heard.

"I don't care if she hears," Angeline wept. "The old witch!"

"Angeline!" Catching sight of Maddie, Ella glared at her. "Get inside 'fore you catch your death. And don't leave a trail'a water on my floor."

Then Nancy sauntered into the room and took in the misery around her with grim satisfaction. "I heared y'all clear out in the hall. What's a'matter in here?"

"You know," Ella said shortly. "You were there when Mistress said she wouldn't buy Royall."

"She sho' was put out," Nancy said. She looked at Angeline. "You see what bein' a slave means now, don'tcha, girl? Means losin' the man you want 'cause Mistress is too spiteful and too tight with a dollar to let you have him."

"I won't lose Royall," Angeline said. "I don't care *what* she says!"

"She tole yo' mama she don't want that boy 'round the place no more, forbid him to set foot on her property," Nancy said.

Angeline's head shot up. "Mama? You didn't tell me that."

Ella gave Nancy a look of fury. "I didn't have time."

Angeline began to cry again. "Royall can't even come here for supper? Oooooh—how I hate that woman!"

"Now do you sees why I want'a be free?" Nancy demanded. "You understands now?"

62

Shaking with anger, Ella swooped down on Nancy. "Get outta my kitchen—'fore I throw you out, you troublesome piece of baggage."

Nancy's eyes narrowed. "Don't you go actin' high and mighty with me, *Miz* Ella, 'cause you's no better'n I am."

"I *said*, get out!"

They were glaring at each other and breathing hard. Maddie thought Nancy was going to jump on Mama and scratch her eyes out. But then Nancy backed down. She flounced to the door, saying over her shoulder, "Some good it does you bein' Mistress's pet. Yo' girl still cain't have her man." And she slammed the door behind her.

"I'm gonna run away," Angeline said.

Ella sighed. "And just where would you go?"

"She and Royall could hide away on a ship," Maddie said.

Ella and Angeline stared at her.

"You could sail out to sea," Maddie continued. "They wouldn't know you were there till it was too late to do anythin' about it."

"Where'd you come up with such nonsense?" Ella demanded.

"From Papa. He wanted to go off on a ship when he was young. Maybe he still does."

Ella looked hard at Maddie. "Papa didn't say that."

"Yes, ma'am, he did."

"Why shouldn't he go if he wants to?" Angeline mused. "Why shouldn't we all go?"

"Angeline, will you listen to yourself?" Ella demanded. "Start tryin' to make sense, girl."

"You keep tellin' us what a good life Mistress gives us," Angeline said, "but I can't even say who I'm gonna keep company with. Soon as Papa gets back, I'm askin' him to help Royall and me get away."

"I forbid it," Ella said.

"Then I'll have to go without your blessing."

Ella started to cry. Maddie watched Angeline go to their mama and embrace her. It was bewildering how quickly everything was changing, how nobody acted the way they always had.

Maddie grabbed her shoes and shawl and crept outside to look for Papa.

Ten

"Will you help us, Papa?" Angeline had told her story and was waiting for his answer.

"You know I will—just don't know how yet." Titus studied the food before him without touching it.

"Everybody eat your supper 'fore it gets cold," Ella ordered.

Obediently they began to eat.

"What makes you so sure Royall's what you want?" Titus asked Angeline. "You ain't known him long."

"I know I love him," Angeline said.

"He feel the same about you?"

"Yes, Papa."

"You're too young to think on marryin' yet."

"I'm nearly fourteen." Angeline's mouth was set in a stubborn line.

"Fourteen's not old enough."

"How old do I have to be?" Angeline demanded.

Titus looked at Ella. "What you think, Mama? Fifteen?"

"Fifteen! But that's more'n a year from now," Angeline protested. "And Mistress said Royall can't even come see me."

"But there's nothin' to say you cain't go to him, is there?" Titus asked gently. "I 'spect nobody here'd mind if you and Maddie went fishin' with him now and again."

"Titus, you know what Mistress meant," Ella said.

"But she *said* Royall cain't come here. And he won't."

The next day, Mister Tate sent Royall to the settlement on Roanoke Island for provisions. Maddie could feel her mama's relief. For one day, at least, Ella wouldn't have to worry about Mistress seeing the boy.

Around mid-morning, Maddie was sweeping the porch when she heard a sound like thunder. Then the earth trembled, and the thunderous noise came again.

Mama and Angeline ran out to the porch, followed quickly by the Mistress and Nancy.

"They've come!" Mistress shrieked. "The bluecoats are here!"

"Them guns ain't firin' close," Nancy said. "Don't see no smoke or nothin'."

"Sounds like it's comin' from over the water," Ella said.

Maddie's heart was beating so loud, she could barely hear the guns for it. She knew the others were as frightened as she was—all except Nancy, whose black eyes blazed with the hope of liberation.

Titus came home and told them to get inside. They all obeyed, even the Mistress, who didn't seem to realize she was taking orders from a slave.

"Titus, where's the firin' comin' from?" she demanded when they had gone back into the kitchen.

" 'Cross the sound. Roanoke Island, maybe."

Angeline's body tensed. She started to speak, but Titus shot her a warning look. Ella reached for her older daughter's hand.

"It's the Yankees?" Mistress paced up and down the kitchen floor. " 'Course it is. We have to leave. Nancy, pack my things. Titus, get the animals ready. Never mind—we'll leave everythin' but the horse." She was so beside herself, Maddie very nearly felt sorry for her.

"Mistress, ain't no ship goin' to the mainland today," Titus told her. "We cain't leave."

"Can't leave? Nonsense!" Mistress looked wildly around the room. "We'll get word to the Master. He'll send a ship."

"How kin we get word to the Master if nobody kin leave?" Titus asked. And then, for the second time in her life, Maddie saw the Mistress cry.

"Nancy, take Mistress upstairs to lie down," Ella said.

Maddie knew her mama was just as scared as the Mistress, but nobody would know it to look at her. Maddie felt a sudden admiration for Ella. And for Angeline, too, who was standing so stiffly beside Papa—worried sick about Royall, but refusing to break down.

"Yes, Nancy, take me upstairs," Mistress said, clinging to her maid's arm. "Titus, guard that door. Don't you let those blue devils in here."

As soon as the Mistress was gone, Angeline ran to the door. Titus stopped her before she could go outside.

"Stay here, daughter. I'll see what I kin find out."

"No, Titus." Ella grabbed his arm. "I won't have you in the middle'a this."

"I'll be careful." He hugged her hard. "And keep this door bolted."

They waited a long time. The guns rumbled, were silent, then rumbled again. Even with all her worries, Ella insisted they finish the morning chores and cook dinner.

It was late afternoon before Titus came back. He had been at the hotel with the few Confederate soldiers still left at Nags Head. The others had gone to fight on Roanoke Island.

67

"So it *is* the Yankees," Ella said, as she pulled off his wet boots and motioned for him to warm himself by the fire.

Titus's eyes were bright. "They say the sound's been full'a gunboats fightin' it out all day. I heard there's Yankee troops on Roanoke Island right now."

"You didn't see Royall?" Angeline asked anxiously.

"No, child," he said gently. "Went by the Tate place, but he's still not back."

Angeline sat down heavily, but she didn't cry.

"Royall can take care'a hisself. He'll be all right."

"But if he's in the middle of the fightin' . . ." Angeline shook her head. "And that crazy old woman thought we'd be safe here!"

For once, Ella didn't even chastise her daughter for not showing the proper respect.

Eleven

It was late when they finally went to bed. Maddie was kept awake for a long time by Angeline's restless movements beside her. She was just drifting into an uneasy sleep when she heard the noise outside. It sounded like an animal scratching at the door—or a Yankee trying to open it? Angeline must have heard it, too, because Maddie felt her sit up suddenly and bolt off the mattress.

"Stay here," Titus said sharply. Maddie saw his shadow move along the wall as he left the room.

Huddled under her blanket, Maddie heard the creak of the back door opening, then whispered voices. Suddenly the room was filled with light and shadows from a candle in the kitchen.

"Y'all can come out now," Titus called softly.

Maddie was the first one into the kitchen, and the first to see Royall standing there. But before she could express her joy at having him back safe and sound, Angeline rushed past her and was swept up into his arms.

Everybody was talking at once. Everybody except Royall—who was standing there beaming while they all hugged him.

"Keep your voices down," Titus warned. "We don't want Mistress hearin'." He pulled out a chair for Royall. "Tell us where you been, son. Looks like you had some day for yourself."

For the first time, Maddie noticed that Royall's clothing was wet and caked with mud.

Angeline's eyes scanned him anxiously. "You hurt?"

"No, just plumb wore out. And mighty glad to be in one piece."

Ella began to stir the dying coals in the fireplace. "Were you on the island when the fightin' started?"

"Yes'm. I heared them guns go off as I tied up the boat. Didn't rightly know what was happenin', so I run into the woods. But the noise kept gettin' louder and closer. Finally, I sez to myself, 'Royall, you done walked smack dab into the midst'a the war.' "

"That was gunboats you heard," Titus said.

Royall nodded. "Don't think I was ever near the worst of it, but I was near enough. Sounded like the world was comin' to an end."

"What if I warm up some fried ham and biscuits for you?" Ella asked.

"That sounds mighty good, Miz Ella. Breakfast was a long time ago."

"So what did you do?" Angeline urged him on.

"Nothin' very brave. Hid out in the woods all day till the guns stopped. When it was finally quiet and dark, I made my way back to the boat. I was scared'a comin' back 'cross the sound 'cause I didn't know what I might run into. So I steered due south."

Royall accepted a cup of coffee from Ella. "It was rainin' hard by then, and there weren't no moon to see by. When I finally come ashore, I was miles from home. And I seen right off that the woods was crawlin' with Confederate soldiers. Had to make my way up to your place real slow, hidin' in the bushes whenever soldiers come by."

"So the Yankees ain't made it to Nags Heads," Titus said.

"We'd a'heared shootin' by now if they had. But I betcha they's on Roanoke Island right now."

"What does it mean, Papa?" Maddie asked, slipping into the chair beside him.

Titus grinned at her. "Could mean that comin' to Nags Head was the best thing ever happened to us."

Maddie woke up late the next morning. The sun would have been high in the sky if the clouds had allowed it to peek through. But the cold, driving rain of the night before persisted. She got dressed and hurried into the kitchen, expecting Ella to be angry with her for sleeping so late.

" 'Mornin', Sleepyhead," Angeline greeted her. She was feeding Pride his breakfast and looked remarkably cheerful after very little sleep.

Ella was ironing one of Mistress's delicate chemises with the heavy irons she'd heated over the fire. "Maddie, hurry with your breakfast so's you can get to your chores. We're runnin' behind today."

She didn't seem angry, Maddie realized with surprise, just anxious to get the work done. Maddie heaped her plate with eggs, ham, and corn pone. "Where's Papa and Royall?"

"Gone to the hotel to hear the news," Ella said. "Angeline, bring me some walnuts from the pantry. I gotta make dye for Mistress's brown dress along with everythin' else."

She was acting like this was an ordinary day, like the Yankees weren't a few miles from their door, Maddie thought. Not that Ella could hide her worry completely.

But she bore it calmly, giving Maddie reason to consider whether her mama wasn't nearly as brave in her own way as Papa was in his.

"Royall didn't go home?"

"No, and I 'spect Mister Tate to come knockin' on the door any time lookin' for him." Ella held the chemise up to inspect it in the light. "We don't need that white man complainin' to Mistress."

"He probably thinks Royall ran into the Yankees," Angeline said, and she winked at Maddie.

They heard shooting off and on all morning, but it wasn't as loud as the day before. Every shot caused Maddie to run to the window to look for Papa, and to see if she could spy men in blue uniforms.

It was mid-afternoon when Royall burst into the kitchen to tell them that he and Titus had seen Confederate soldiers coming back from Roanoke Island.

"Not many, though, and a sorry sight they was," he said joyously. "They's been whooped, Miz Ella, most of 'em captured by the Yankees. The rest is packin' up to leave Nags Head."

"Where's my husband?" Ella asked quietly.

"He sez to tell you he'll be 'long directly." Then to everybody's surprise, Royall walked over and planted a kiss on Ella's cheek. "Hope you don't think I'm bein' too bold, Miz Ella, but if my mama was alive, I'd be kissin' her about now."

A little later someone pounded on the front door. Ella opened it to Sergeant Jakes and two of his men. Their uniforms were muddy and torn. They looked exhausted.

"I'm here to see your mistress," the sergeant said.

"Is it bad news?" Mistress hurried down the stairs and

brushed past Maddie, Angeline, and Royall without seeing them.

"The Yankees have Roanoke Island, ma'am," the sergeant said in a weary voice. "Most'a our men was taken prisoner, the ones not shot outright. We don't have the troops to hold Nags Head."

The Mistress's face reflected her despair, but Nancy's eyes glittered at the sergeant's words. Maddie half expected her to run out the door to welcome the Yankees.

"General Wise is movin' his troops outta Nags Head 'fore the enemy arrives," the sergeant went on. "Sent me to ask if you'd like to go with us. I don't see you have much choice," he added. " 'Less you want to wait and serve tea to Burnside's men when they get here."

"So they've finally come," the Mistress said with unexpected calm. Then she gave Royall a hard stare. "What are you doin' here, boy? Ella, didn't I say this slave wasn't to set foot on my property?"

"Yes, Mistress."

"Then get him outta here," she said coldly. "And find that shiftless husband of yours and tell him to get the animals ready. Nancy, see to the packin' of my trunks."

"We can't be takin' all your baggage and livestock," Sergeant Jakes said. "Just the horses and whatever your people can carry."

"But my gowns and the silver, and the portrait of my sons—"

"You'll have to leave 'em," the soldier said curtly. He replaced his cap. "We'll be movin' out in an hour, ma'am."

The next hour was a blur when Maddie tried to remember it later. While she packed their few clothes,

Titus saddled the one horse, and Ella and Angeline buried Mistress's silver tea service and dinnerware.

"You buried 'em in the sand?" Titus asked Ella.

"That's what Mistress said to do."

Titus began to laugh. "The way this sand shifts, she'll never find 'em again."

When Maddie brought their bundles of clothing into the kitchen, Titus told her to take the quilts and blankets off their mattresses and pack them too. Then he sent Angeline into the pantry to gather up enough food for a couple of days.

Ella looked at him sharply. "What are you up to, Titus?"

He was filling a burlap sack with candles, plates, and a small cooking pot. "We're gonna be spendin' a day or two in the woods."

Ella took the sack from him and set it firmly on the floor. "I'm not goin' anywhere till you tell me what's goin' on."

"No time to talk now. I'll tell you everythin' once we're away from here."

Angeline came out of the pantry carrying food. "Papa, are we runnin' away?"

"Keep your voice down," Titus warned.

"But where's Royall?" Angeline demanded. "I won't go without him."

"Royall's comin'. He'll join us soon as he kin."

"But—"

"No more questions." Titus slung the food sack over his shoulder. "Go tell your sister we're ready to leave."

Twelve

L ater on, when Maddie thought about the day she and
her family ran for freedom, it would strike her as odd
how commonplace it had seemed. In fact, they didn't run
at all; while Nancy and Mistress were upstairs packing,
Titus and Ella and their children just walked out the
kitchen door and disappeared into the woods.

Each had a bundle of clothing, bedding, or food.
Angeline carried Pride in her arms. They walked swiftly,
without speaking, as Titus had directed them to, until
they were deep in the woods. Finally, Titus told them they
could rest.

Angeline was the first to speak. "Papa, where's
Royall?"

"Headed for Roanoke Island."

"Didn't he get enough of the place yesterday?" Ella's
tone was brittle. "All right, husband, tell me everythin' or
I'm not takin' another step into these woods."

"This mornin' Royall and me come up on two slaves
tryin' to get to Roanoke Island. They'd heared the island
was captured and was hopin' the Yankees would take 'em
in. Used to be talk in the cabins of slaves runnin' after the
Yankees when they'd won a battle, and the bluecoats
treatin' 'em good."

"I don't wanta hear about talk in the cabins," Ella
said.

"Then we saw rebel soldiers comin' back. They was in sorry shape. One of 'em told us he'd seen a little boat headin' from here to Roanoke Island. It was filled with colored folks singin' about the Promised Land."

"Did the soldier shoot 'em, Papa?" Maddie asked.

"No, little girl. He just watched 'em row to the island. And he saw this Yankee soldier standin' on the bank'a the island wavin' the little boat in. And when the boat reached the island, that Yankee soldier slid down the bank and helped 'em pull their boat to shore."

"Sounds to me like somebody was havin' fun with two nosy slaves," Ella said. "Or else a Yankee soldier was in need of a boat."

"Ella, this man was hurt and sick at heart," Titus said. "He weren't in no mind to be playin' with us. The Yankees are takin' in runaways, sho' enough. Royall and me decided Roanoke Island's where we need to go."

"But why didn't he wait for us?" Angeline asked.

"He's gone to see if it's safe 'fore we take you women and children there."

"He coulda told me."

"Wasn't time, daughter, with the rebel soldiers fixin' to leave. A few more minutes and we'd have had half the Confederate Army to see we didn't run nowhere."

"But why would white men help us?" Ella asked. "Most likely, they'll meet us and put guns to our heads. Reckon we'll know if Royall never gets back."

"Mama!"

"Quit your frettin', Angeline," Titus said. "We'll see Royall sometime tomorrow. He knows where to find us."

"And, meantime, we're to sleep out in the wet and cold?" Ella said. "What if the children get sick?"

"They kin stand one night without a roof over their heads." Titus winked at Maddie. "Cain't you, girl?"

"Yessir, Papa."

"What about Nancy?" Ella said suddenly. "We should'a let her come with us."

"We couldn't have her disappear without Mistress knowin' what we was up to," Titus said. "She'll find her chance to run if she's a mind to."

It was late the next day when Royall came back. Angeline ran through the tangle of vines and bushes to meet him.

"What took you so long?" she demanded.

"Couldn't leave for the island till General Wise and his men was gone," Royall said. They all crowded around him. "They's so mad at the slaves for turnin' traitor—that's what they called it—they'd have shot me on sight."

"They've left Nags Head then," Titus said.

"They's left and the Yankees has arrived." Royall grinned. "Didn't you see the fire last night?"

"We saw." Ella's voice was heavy. "Yankees burnin' everythin' in their path."

"No, ma'am, it weren't the Yankees," Royall said. "That was rebel soldiers—burnin' down the hotel 'fore they left so's the Yankees couldn't use it."

Titus looked troubled. "What's the sense of burnin' down a good buildin' outta spite?"

"I don't rightly know," Royall said. "All's I know is these here banks is about the safest place there is for a slave."

"Roanoke Island too?" Titus asked.

"Most specially Roanoke Island." Royall's grin spread.

"Yankees is settin' up tents for runaways, givin' 'em food and clothes. They *wants* us there."

"You saw this with your own eyes?" Ella demanded.

"Yes, ma'am, I did. And you know what else? The army's hirin' the men to build a fort, and they's payin' 'em a wage."

"Paying wages to a slave?" Ella looked incredulous.

"Yes'm, Miz Ella, I swears it on my mama's grave," Royall said solemnly. "Only they's not slaves no more. They's free men. And they's paid cash money like free men."

"Just think, Ella!" Titus exclaimed. "We kin save to buy us a farm. Wouldn't you like livin' on land that belongs to you?"

"I can't rightly think how that would be," Ella admitted. "It would be like you and me bein' the Master and Mistress."

"Naw, Miz Ella," Royall said. "Ain't gonna be no more Master and Mistress. Just gonna be all of us workin' together."

Ella looked bewildered. "Wonder where the Mistress is now," she murmured. "Maybe they burned her house too."

"Mistress gonna be fine," Titus said. "You spent your whole life fussin' over her, wife. Time you had a life of your own. You hear me?"

"I hear," Ella said. Her eyes came to rest on Maddie. "Anyhow, there's nothin' says these children have to starve just 'cause they're runnin' away. Angeline, untie that bundle with the last of the corn pone," she said with some of her old energy. "We'll have supper 'fore we leave—'less you men can't wait that long for the Promised Land."

"I figger a man should go to the Promised Land with his belly full," Titus said with a grin. He reached for his wife and hugged her.

"Behave yourself, Titus," Ella chided him. But she smiled a little as she cut the corn pone into squares for supper.

PART THREE

Roanoke Island

FEBRUARY 1862–MAY 1865

Thirteen

Now that the excitement of capturing Roanoke Island was over, the Union troops had more mundane duties to perform. Luckily, the retreating Confederate soldiers had left their quarters standing—more than twenty wooden buildings that would now house General Burnside's men. But there was a fort and docks to build—a necessity if they wanted to hold on to the island, but one that didn't tickle the imaginations of young men who had joined the army to be soldiers.

Soon most of the troops would be moving out to do battle on the mainland. The restless men waited impatiently for that day to come. For all its natural beauty, Roanoke Island was too isolated, and too quiet now that the fighting was done.

Gil Robbins had guard duty that night, but he was finding it hard to stay awake. There was always the danger of a sniper—some stray Johnny Reb just waiting to start firing at them—but Gil figured the odds of that happening were little to none. The island had been combed for rebs, and was now about as safe as any place in the South.

Gil could hear his buddies back at camp, laughing and fighting good-naturedly over a game of cards. He wished he were with them, instead of being stuck in the middle of the woods alone. His feet were wet, and his legs ached from standing so long. It was against regulation, but who would know if he took a short rest?

Gil sat down and reached for the harmonica in his pocket. He had played only a few notes of "Darling Nelly Gray" when he heard a sound in the bushes nearby.

Afraid that his sergeant would find him resting instead of guarding, Gil leaped to his feet and grabbed his rifle. The harmonica fell unnoticed to the ground.

The sounds of movement in the undergrowth became louder, and Gil's heart began to thump. He pointed his rifle toward the disturbance and prepared to fire.

Royall was leading the way through the dense growth of cypress, holly, and pine to the Yankee soldiers' camp. Ella and the children followed single file behind him, with Titus at the rear.

"We's nearly there," Royall whispered over his shoulder. "Hear 'em laughin'?" He pushed aside a tree branch and saw the barrel of a rifle glistening in the moonlight—a rifle pointed straight at his head.

"Don't shoot!" Royall cried out instinctively, not knowing who held the weapon or whether the man would heed his words or not.

"Who goes there?" Gil barked. Then, hearing more movement behind his target, he added, "How many are with you?"

"Uh—just one fam'ly," Royall stammered. "I got women and younguns with me. We's runnin' away from our masters."

The bright moonlight fell on the figures of two women, another man, and a couple of children. "Oh, boy," Gil muttered as he lowered his rifle. "Not more of you." The captain was going to love this!

The young bluecoat didn't act especially glad to see

them, Maddie thought, as she and her family trudged behind him through the dark woods. But then, he hadn't shot them either. The sight of that rifle had scared her into wishing she was back at River Bend—still a slave, but at least alive.

The soldier led them into a clearing lit with campfires. There were other bluecoats—a lot of them!—sitting around the fires. When they saw Maddie and her family, they stopped talking and laughing. Maddie felt Ella's fingers dig into her shoulder.

"Wait here," the soldier said. He disappeared into one of the wooden buildings beyond the campfires.

Conversation rose up again among the bluecoats, but now it was whispered. Maddie looked at their faces. She saw curiosity in some—and something more disturbing in others. Maddie couldn't hear what the soldiers were saying, but she sensed that all were not happy to see the new arrivals.

When the young soldier came back, he was followed by an older man in uniform who had one arm in a sling.

"This is Sergeant Taylor," the young man told them.

"So you're contraband." The sergeant's voice was gruff. But his light eyes under bushy gray brows were not unkind as they swept over Maddie and the rest of them.

"Sir?" Titus didn't understand what the old soldier had said.

"Contraband. That's what the government calls runaways. You ran from your masters, didn't you?"

"Yessir," Titus said.

"If we let you stay, are you willin' to work?" the soldier asked brusquely.

"I been workin' hard all my life," Titus replied. "Reckon I'll be workin' till the day I die."

"All right," the sergeant said. "You'll get food and materials to set up a tent for yourselves. We'll pay you eight dollars a month to help us build a fort and docks. Sound agreeable so far?"

Titus grinned, his worry replaced by pure joy. "Yessir, mighty agreeable."

The sergeant's craggy face softened. "You want a job too?" he asked Royall.

"Yessir, I do."

"Then come on and I'll sign you up."

They followed him into a building that was filled with crates. He sat down at a lone table and reached for a pen.

"What's your names?"

Titus repeated each of their names carefully.

"Don't suppose you have last names," the sergeant said when he had written it all down.

"No, sir," Titus said. "Slaves ain't allowed but one name."

"But you aren't slaves anymore, are you?" The older man watched the truth of what he said begin to dawn on them. "So you're gonna need second names. Some of the contraband are takin' their old masters' names."

"My master's named Tate," Royall said with a grin. "Just sign me up as Royall Tate."

"And you?" the sergeant said to Titus. "You gonna take your master's name?"

"No, sir, don't rightly see how my fam'ly and me could do that." Titus frowned thoughtfully. He looked at Ella. "My daddy's name was Henry. How you feel about Henry for your name?"

"Henry's fine," Ella said softly.

"Then Henry it is." The sergeant scribbled down the name and looked up. His eyes came to rest on Maddie's solemn face. "That meet with your approval, young lady?"

Maddie nodded jerkily. She was too nervous to speak to the strange white man.

"You don't have to be afraid," he said as he studied her. "I'm not gonna bite you."

"Or hitch me to a plow like a mule?" Maddie whispered.

"Maddie!" Ella yanked on Maddie's arm.

But the old sergeant didn't seem offended. In fact, he threw back his head and laughed—a deep belly-shaking laugh that made Maddie smile, even though Ella still glared at her.

"No, child," Sergeant Taylor said, still chuckling. "Nor that either. Little girls should be looked after, not worked like farm animals."

And even Ella relaxed a little.

Several families were already living in the nearby camp that had been set up for runaways. Maddie looked around in wonderment as they followed the sergeant into the camp. Tents lined the edge of the clearing. Campfires glowed. Smells of roasted pork and coffee filled the air. Most of the people, freed slaves like herself, smiled as Maddie and her family walked past.

"Eventually, you can build yourselves a more permanent shelter," the sergeant told Titus. "Meanwhile, pick out a tent site. I'll send some men down with supplies."

"See, Ella, it wasn't all nonsense," Titus said later. They sat alone by the fire outside their newly raised tent. "Did you hear the sergeant? We're gonna have us a home of our own."

"Yes, Titus, I heard," Ella said softly. She leaned over to stir the dying embers, savoring their remaining warmth.

Fourteen

It was peculiar living in a house with canvas walls and no floor. But after she got used to it, Maddie decided she liked their new home. The only furnishings were straw-filled mattresses and wooden crates for storing food and clothing, so housekeeping was no chore at all.

Of course, there was no privacy either. Royall had his own small tent next door, but all of Maddie's family lived in the one room. And when it rained, there was no way to keep the dampness out. Titus dug a trench around the tent so most of the water ran off, but mold built up on the canvas, and the odor clung to the fabric long after the rain had ended.

Nobody complained about the inconveniences. Even Ella had stopped voicing her suspicions and fears. And every evening around the fire, Titus and Royall drew plans in the dirt of the houses they dreamed of building.

Gone were the days when the family dined on fresh meat and vegetables from the Big House. Now they ate what the army gave them: salt beef and pork, hard bread, beans, and coffee.

The men left early each morning to join the others who were building an earthen fort on the northern end of the island. Ella and Angeline still rose before the sun was up to build the fire, cook breakfast, and pack dinners for their men to take with them.

It was a friendly community, made up of people who were eager to share their good fortune with one another. Women often stopped by to chat with Ella in the afternoons, to bring a pot of bean soup, and to talk about the progress their men were making on the fort. After supper families would visit together, the children playing in the gathering dusk while the grown-ups talked about the future, about the dream they all shared: to own a little piece of land with a real house on it.

Each day more runaways arrived. By the time the troops left for the mainland in March, several hundred people were living in tents and makeshift huts in the contraband camp.

Maddie was in the woods near the army camp gathering yaupon leaves for tea the day the soldiers left for New Bern. She saw Gil among the troops preparing to move out. Although she knew that some of the soldiers didn't want the runaways on the island, she hoped Gil didn't feel that way. He was the first Yankee she had ever met—her first contact with the people who were giving them a new life—and she wanted him to like her. She waved frantically to catch his attention.

When he noticed her standing at the edge of the woods, her arm swinging wildly, Gil grinned at her and waved back. That was the last time she ever saw him.

Sergeant Taylor found her sitting on the steps of one of the deserted buildings after the soldiers left. "So how you like your new home?" he asked.

"I like it just fine." Maddie was still shy, but no longer afraid of the tall white man with the gruff voice. "You not leavin' with the others?"

"Not just yet." He held out his bandaged arm. "Wouldn't be much good to 'em with this broken wing."

"Where they goin'?"

"Into North Carolina, to send more of them rebel boys runnin'. Wish I could be there," he added pensively.

"I'm glad they're leavin'," Maddie said, before she thought. Then she gave him an anxious look. "I mean, they don't seem to like us much."

The sergeant studied her face. "Some of 'em may not," he said. "But they don't know you, do they? Probably never even met colored folks before. And some of 'em are just mean. The army's got its share of bad apples, same as anywhere else."

"Well, I'm glad you're stayin'," Maddie said.

He grinned. "That's good to know, 'cause you're gonna see a lotta me. I'm in charge of you folks."

"What does that mean?"

"I'm supposed to help you get settled and see you have everything you need. There's other people who've heard about you and want to help too. We just got in a shipment of things for you."

The next morning soldiers brought a lot of wooden crates and barrels to the contraband camp. The camp's residents put down their brooms and buckets and gathered around the sergeant.

"There's people in the North who want to help you," Sergeant Taylor said. "Like the missionary societies. And the abolitionists. They're folks who believe slavery is wrong and want to see it done away with. They've collected money and clothes and other things you'll need."

Maddie couldn't tear her eyes from the stack of crates and barrels beside him. There was no telling what wondrous things they held.

The sergeant told the other soldiers to begin unpacking

the containers. "Just come up here when I call your names," he said to the waiting crowd.

Maddie watched as the head of each family was called forward, one by one, and the soldiers passed out the contents of the crates and barrels. There was new bedding to replace ragged blankets, seeds for planting, farm tools, and cooking utensils. There were bolts of cloth, leather shoes, dresses, and trousers. Some of the clothing was not new, but it was all clean and in good condition. Maddie remembered the red mittens with the holes in the thumbs that Master had given her last Christmas. She was sure Papa remembered too.

Finally Maddie heard Sergeant Taylor call Papa's name. Titus Henry. She loved that name! And Papa stepped forward proudly when he heard it.

The sergeant gave Titus blankets, a kettle, and a hoe. Ella had to come help with the other things: a bolt of blue calico, tin plates, and seeds for planting a garden. There was a shirt for Pride and new trousers for Papa. But best of all were the dresses for Mama, Angeline, and Maddie.

Maddie could hardly believe it when Papa handed her the dress. It was the first store-bought piece of clothing she had ever owned. Little pink flowers danced across a background of light brown. There were tiny pearl buttons down the front and a row of pink ribbon and lace at the throat. It was the most beautiful dress Maddie had ever seen.

After the soldiers were gone, Maddie folded her dress carefully and put it away in the crate at the foot of her mattress. She would wear it someday for a special occasion. But for now, it was enough just to know that it was hers.

Fifteen

Summer came early to Roanoke Island that year. By mid-April Maddie and Angeline had taken to moving their mattresses out under the stars on clear nights to escape the sweltering tent. Unfortunately, the swamplands on the island attracted swarms of mosquitoes, whose relentless attacks made the nights even more miserable. But there was nothing to do about it except rub the bites with onion or walnut leaves and endure.

There were almost a thousand people living in the contraband camp now. The camp, in fact, had become very nearly a city; with its own laws, as laid down by the army, its own church, and its own hospital.

The church was nothing more than a collection of pine-slab benches set among the trees, with a crate for a pulpit. An army surgeon had set up the hospital in one of the barracks buildings, intending it for ill and wounded soldiers; but as the population of runaway slaves increased, so did their use of the hospital.

In addition to their daily chores of cooking, washing, cleaning, and caring for Pride, Angeline and Maddie also worked in the hospital. The surgeon and medics had left with the other troops, but there were healers who cared for the sick and midwives who delivered the babies born at the camp.

Angeline was an excellent nurse, which didn't surprise

Maddie. She was used to seeing her sister do well at nearly everything she tried. The ill seemed to take comfort just from having Angeline nearby. She was the one they called when they wanted a sip of water or gentle hands to wipe their brows.

Maddie was better with the babies. From the beginning, she gravitated toward Sister Melba, who had gradually taken over the hospital. It was from Sister Melba that Maddie learned how to bathe the newborns and wrap them in clean muslin for their mothers' waiting arms.

Sister Melba was old but very strong, and taller than most of the men. Her skin was the blackest black Maddie had ever seen. That was because her granny came from a place called Africa, she explained to Maddie. The people in this place lived in tribes. Those in Sister Melba's tribe were all exceptionally tall and thin, their skin the color of burned wood after the fire had died.

Sister Melba conversed with the spirits of the dead as easily as she spoke to the living. She believed in talismans and omens, premonitions and dreams. She never smiled. She never stopped by a neighbor's tent to visit. She just worked at the hospital—twelve, fourteen, sometimes sixteen hours a day. People in the camp thought she was peculiar. Some were a little afraid of her. But still they found her strangely compelling. When she looked you straight in the face with her hypnotic black eyes, and said you would be all right, you believed her.

Even though their days were busy, and there was always work to be done, Maddie and Angeline had more free time than they had ever had at the plantation. Often in the afternoon, the sisters would explore the woods, picking flowers and herbs as they walked, or go fishing in the sound. One of their neighbors, who had lived his whole life on the banks, helped Maddie make a fishing net and taught her how to spread it between poles in the sound to catch shad. In the evening, Angeline spent all her time with Royall, who had long since been accepted as a member of the family.

"I think it's time you learned to read," Angeline said to Royall one night as they sat talking after supper.

Royall looked surprised. Then he grinned. "Cain't you do the readin' for both of us?"

"You're a free man now," Angeline said. She ducked into the tent to get the Bible and one of Ella's precious sheets of paper. "You need to be able to sign your name and read what you're signin'."

Royall sighed, and Maddie gave him a sympathetic look. It wasn't often that Angeline dug in her heels; but when she did, she was bound and determined to have her way.

"I'll write your name, and I want you to copy it," Angeline told him. "See, this is an *R*. This is an *O*. This is a *Y* . . ."

Angeline worked with Royall every evening for a week, teaching him the alphabet and how to print his name. But the lessons didn't go well. Royall was smart, but he didn't seem to remember anything Angeline taught him. Angeline soon became frustrated.

"You aren't tryin'," she accused him one evening.

"You 'spect too much too fast," he shot back.

"You don't wanta learn 'cause it wasn't your idea."

"I wanta learn." Royall glared at her. "But I don't think you're the one to teach me."

Angeline couldn't have looked more shocked and hurt if he had slapped her. "If that's how you feel, we'll find you another teacher then." She whipped around to Maddie. "*You* teach him."

Maddie opened her mouth to protest, but Titus cut her off.

"Sounds like a right smart idea, daughter," he said to Angeline. "Could be you and Royall are too close. What with you wantin' him to do good, and him wantin' too much to please you, neither of you kin give it your best. How you feel about Maddie bein' your teacher, son?"

"I feels fine about it," Royall said grimly.

"Then, Maddie, you kin start tomorrow night," Titus said.

During the evening lessons, Angeline usually found a reason to be inside the tent or visiting a neighbor. Which was just as well, Maddie thought. When her sister was around, Royall couldn't think about anything but Angeline. But when Angeline wasn't there to distract him, he learned quickly. In three weeks, he was printing his name and sounding out passages from the Bible.

"You're a born teacher," Titus told Maddie one night after Royall had gone to his tent. "You make Royall feel real proud'a hisself."

Maddie beamed. Suddenly she felt confident enough to share her secret with him. "I always wanted to teach the children on the row to read and do sums," she admitted. "I was thinkin' maybe I could teach the children here."

"That's a fine idea," Titus said. He smoothed her hair with his rough hand. "We'll talk about it some more. But it's gettin' late now, so off to bed with you."

The next morning Maddie was washing clothes in a tub outside the tent while Ella and Angeline visited an ailing neighbor. Pride, who was now a sturdy boy of almost three, was lying on his belly watching a caterpillar inch through the grass.

The sun was already beating down. Maddie wiped the sweat from her face. As usual, she had forgotten Ella's reminder to wear a bonnet.

"Pride, I'm goin' inside a minute," she called to the boy. "Don't you run off."

"I won't," he said, his attention still focused on the furry worm.

Maddie went inside the tent and mopped her face with a wet rag. She found her sunbonnet and tied the sashes defiantly under her chin. But what she really needed was a drink of cold water from the well.

She picked up the water bucket outside the tent and turned to call Pride—but he wasn't there. She looked everywhere for him: behind the washtub, where he some-times hid from her; in back of the tent; under the wet sheets draped over nearby bushes. Then she panicked.

Maddie ran to Royall's tent and stuck her head inside. Pride wasn't there either. Where could he have gone so fast? Why hadn't she stayed with him? He was just a baby, she berated herself, too little to have been left alone. Mama would have her hide. If anything happened to him . . .

Maddie banished the thought from her mind and raced to the next tent to ask if they had seen him.

That was when she heard her name. A soft, high-pitched voice that could have only been Pride's was call-ing to her. Weak with relief, she followed the voice into the woods.

He hadn't wandered far, just into the bushes a few yards from camp. When he saw her, he giggled. "Maddie, come look. Look what I find."

"Honestly, Pride, you scared me half to death. Don't you ever do that again," she fussed as she walked toward him.

Then she saw it. A small brown snake lay coiled at Pride's feet.

"Pride, honey, don't move," Maddie said in a voice that didn't sound like her own. She edged toward him.

"What is it, Maddie?"

"It's a snake," Maddie said softly. "You can't touch it 'cause it'll bite you. Just stand real still."

"He wanta play," Pride protested. "Won't bite—"

Maddie grabbed the boy and jerked him away—just as the snake struck at Pride's leg. Not understanding what had happened, but knowing that he didn't like the way his sister was treating him, Pride began to howl.

"Hush, baby," Maddie murmured, as she pushed through the bushes toward the tent with Pride in her arms. "You're not hurt. Hush, now."

"Lemme go! Down, put me down!" He was screaming in fury.

"Ssssh. It's all right," Maddie soothed.

"Maddie?"

Ella and Angeline stood in front of their tent. The look of anguish on Ella's face when she saw her screaming son filled Maddie with new guilt and shame.

"He's not hurt—just scared," Maddie hurried to assure her mother.

"What happened?" Ella reached for Pride and hugged him tightly.

"He found a copperhead—"

"Sweet Jesus!"

"He wasn't bitten, Mama. He was out in the woods—"

"Alone?" Ella's eyes bored into Maddie. "You were

s'posed to watch him. Can't I trust you with your brother for a few minutes?"

"Mama, no harm was done," Angeline said. Her eyes filled with pity as they came to rest on Maddie's stricken face.

"No thanks to your sister," Ella snapped. She rocked Pride gently in her arms until he stopped sobbing. Then she turned back to Maddie, who was staring miserably at the ground.

"I knew we should'a been harder on you," Ella said in a cold voice. "But your papa said no, life was hard enough without us addin' to it. He spoiled you, and I let him. And 'cause of that, my baby nearly died. I'll never trust you with him again."

Ella disappeared into the tent. Maddie stood frozen.

"Maddie, she didn't mean it," Angeline said. "You know how she is about Pride. It wasn't your fault. Coulda happened with any of us here."

Maddie shook her head. It wouldn't have happened if Angeline had been there. Angeline could be trusted. She wouldn't have left Pride alone.

"Honey, please don't look like that," Angeline pleaded. "Come inside. She'll get over it."

"No, she won't," Maddie said. "She won't ever get over it."

Ella never mentioned the incident again, and neither did Maddie. But it stood like a wall between them—a constant reminder to Maddie of how she had failed, and how that failure would never be forgiven.

Maddie had always known that she wasn't Mama's favorite. But she had hoped that her mama had enough tenderness inside for there to be a *little* left over for her.

Now she knew that wasn't so, and it came close to breaking her heart.

Then she began to accept it, as she had accepted all painful and inevitable circumstances of her life. Aunt Lucy always said, "If you don't have a horse to ride, you rides a cow. Life's mostly makin' do." So Maddie made do. She cherished the affection she got from Titus, Angeline, and Royall. And she tried not to mind that there was no place left for her in her mama's heart.

.

Sixteen

Maddie's favorite day of the week was Sunday, because that was when they all dressed up in their best clothes and gathered at the church in the woods to hear Brother Earl preach. Brother Earl had been a free man before coming to Roanoke Island. He had traveled throughout the North and the South spreading the Gospel, but it was on Roanoke Island, he said, that he had finally found his flock.

Brother Earl was as tall and skinny as a pole for running beans. He always dressed like a preacher. Even in the middle of the week, Maddie would see him walking through the camp in his good black suit.

Everybody loved Brother Earl. They loved hearing him preach, for he was a powerful speaker. And they loved gathering in their woodland church, with its sweet smell of pine and its rough benches, to celebrate their freedom.

Maddie wore her store-bought dress with the pink flowers and pearl buttons on Sundays. She always felt good in that dress, even though it was already a little short and beginning to feel tight at the neck. Since her twelfth birthday that spring, Maddie had been shooting up an inch at a time. She was nearly as tall as Angeline now.

One Sunday morning in June, Maddie hurried to the church ahead of her family. It was her day to bring flowers, and she wanted to have them there before services.

A lot of folks had already arrived, to visit a little before Brother Earl began to preach. But there was one face in the crowd that Maddie didn't recognize. A sharp-chinned, light brown face belonging to a boy about her age. He was staring at her—rudely, she thought, because he never smiled; he just followed her around with his big eyes stuck to her like a cocklebur.

Maddie fussed with the swamp roses and blanketflowers until she was sure they looked just right. Then she joined Angeline in the front row. The boy sat two benches over from her, and he kept on staring—right through Brother Earl's preaching.

It was a good sermon. All about sinners being goats, and the righteous being sheep. And about how on Judgment Day the Lord would separate the sheep from the goats and keep them with Him forever. But Maddie had a hard time listening with that boy's eyes fixed on her.

When the sermon was over, they all stood to sing.

O Freedom, O Freedom, O Freedom over me!
Before I'll be a slave
I'll be buried in my grave,
And go home to my Lord
And be free.

While everybody was singing and clapping, Maddie stole another look at the young stranger. He was still watching her!

Maddie decided she'd had about enough of this rude boy. After services, she marched over to where he sat and returned his stare.

"My name's Maddie Henry," she said. "That's my family I was sitting with."

The boy studied his bare feet. His clothes were none

too clean, patched and repatched, and he looked like he'd missed a lot of meals.

Suddenly Maddie felt sorry for him. He must have just arrived on the island and hadn't gotten new clothes yet. She wondered if Mama would mind her inviting him home for dinner.

"Don't you have a name?" she asked when he didn't speak.

He raised his eyes then. They were large and black— beautiful eyes in that pinched, somber face that needed more meat on it. "Yeah, I gotta name," he said softly.

"So what is it?"

"Zebedee."

"Zebedee what?"

"Just Zebedee."

"You can have another name now, you know. Any name you want. My papa picked Henry 'cause that was his daddy's name. What's your papa's name?"

"Don't have no papa." He lowered his eyes again.

"You gotta mama?"

He shook his head but wouldn't look at her.

"Did you come here by yourself?"

"I come with them." He jerked his head in the direction of an old couple who stood talking to Brother Earl. They were as poorly dressed as Zebedee, but they looked better fed.

"You share a tent with 'em?"

"Till I builds me a house." He raised his eyes and they met Maddie's. "You sho' ask a powerful lotta questions, don'tcha?"

Maddie thought she saw a glint of humor in those black eyes. She realized she was being teased. "Just one more, Zebedee," she said saucily. "You wanta come home with me for dinner?"

As it turned out, Ella had already asked the old couple—who were named Doc and Martha—so Zebedee tagged along. He didn't seem to care if he was there or not, but Maddie saw his eyes grow big when Ella set the squirrel pie and corn dumplings on the crate in front of him. He devoured his dinner like a starved dog.

Ella must have noticed because she kept refilling his plate without even asking if he wanted more. Finally he shook his head. "Had all I kin hold, but it was mighty fine food," he mumbled.

Maddie learned a little about Zebedee by listening to Doc and Martha talk during the meal. They had been owned by a man named Bryant down at Edenton, wherever that was. Master Bryant was rich enough to own twenty slaves, and mean as the devil himself. He'd owned Zebedee's mama, too, until she'd died of the fever three summers ago.

Maddie glanced at Zebedee when Doc mentioned his mama, but Zebedee kept his head lowered over his plate like he hadn't heard.

"Master'd beat a slave within an inch of his life," Doc said. "Sometimes beyond. I seen two men die under his whip, and another crippled for life."

"Don't think about that now," Martha urged him.

Doc frowned. "Me and Martha had six chilluns. Three died, the other three was sold to the slave trader."

The grief on the old woman's face as she listened to her husband caused a painful tightening in Maddie's chest.

"We's away from there now," Martha said. "We's found heaven on earth, sho' as I'm born."

"Amen," Titus said quietly.

"Amen," Doc echoed.

After they'd washed and dried the dinner dishes, Maddie and Angeline came back to sit with the others. Maddie was surprised to see that Zebedee was still there. She had thought he'd disappear as soon as his belly was full.

"You seen the island yet?" she asked him.

"Nothin' 'cept the church and this here camp."

"If you want, I'll show you where there's good fishing."

He clammed up again on the way to the sound. Maddie pointed out yaupon trees and herbs that were hard to find and a fat blue-tailed lizard, but Zebedee remained silent. When they reached the water, she showed him where she spread her nets.

"You can catch more shad with a net than you'll ever eat," she told him. When he still didn't say anything, she sat down on the bank and started throwing pinecones into the water.

"How old are you, anyhow?" she asked after a while.

"Cain't rightly say. Martha 'members the winter I wuz born, but she cain't recollect how many winters ago that wuz."

"I figger you're about my age. Twelve. That's mighty young to be runnin' off on your own."

Zebedee shrugged. "I been on my own a long time."

"Was it dangerous when you ran away?"

"I reckon. 'Specially when he set the dogs on us." Suddenly Zebedee's eyes sparkled, and he actually smiled. "But we wuz too smart for them ole hounds. We rubbed onions on our feet and legs, and them dogs wuz runnin' in circles tryin' to pick up our scent."

"That was pretty smart," Maddie said. "What woulda happened if he'd caught you?"

"He'd have beat me," Zebedee said matter-of-factly. "Or let the dogs rip me up."

"Did he ever beat you?"

"Some." Zebedee stretched out on the grassy bank and squinted against the sun. "You sho' do have a lotta questions, Maddie Henry."

Maddie smiled, pleased that he had used her name. "Way I see it, that's the only way to learn what you wanta know."

Seventeen

That summer Maddie started a school for the children. Each weekday morning after their chores were done, about twenty children gathered at the church for their lessons.

Maddie had few teaching materials. Just her mama's Bible—which Ella let her use reluctantly, and then only after Titus talked to her—and a piece of rough lumber that Maddie wrote on with charcoal sticks from the fire.

School attendance was sporadic, since the children were often needed to work at home. And many children at the camp didn't come at all. But Maddie was encouraged when some of the same faces showed up morning after morning.

Maddie's one disappointment was that she couldn't convince Zebedee to come to school. As the summer progressed, they spent more and more time together, often going out to fish in the afternoons or to gather bits of lumber for Zebedee to use for building his house. Maddie had become fond of the boy. More than anything, she wanted him to learn to read.

"I'm too old for that stuff," he told her.

"George is older'n you and he's comin'."

"Maybe George's got the time," Zebedee said patiently. "I ain't. I gotta build me a house 'fore winter."

Since Zebedee found time to wander over the island with her, Maddie knew that wasn't the real reason he refused to come to school. But she couldn't pry his reasons out of him.

Besides teaching her pupils to read and write and do sums, Maddie also read to them from the Bible. They dearly loved stories of pharaohs and kings, and she suspected that some came just to hear the stories.

One morning she was reading aloud the story of David and Goliath when she became aware of whispering among the children. She looked up to see Martha sitting down on one of the empty benches. Surprised, but pleased, Maddie kept on reading.

Gradually, other older people began to come to the school. By August, Maddie had nearly fifty students gathering at the church each day, and she could no longer handle it alone.

"I'll help you," Angeline told her.

"Can't spare you ever' day," Ella said quickly. "We got work to do here, too."

"I'll get up earlier and do chores 'fore I go," Angeline said.

"I'll work harder in the afternoon," Maddie promised.

"Let 'em do it, Ella," Titus said. "It's a good thing they wanta do."

Ella never actually agreed to the plan, but Angeline began to join Maddie every morning at the school. And the number of pupils kept growing.

One morning in late August, Maddie and Angeline were hurrying to class. Maddie glanced up at the black clouds overhead. "Looks like we're in for a good'n," she muttered, thinking of the dampness that remained in their tent from the last rain.

"Maybe we'll have time for one lesson 'fore it starts," Angeline said.

Most of the students were already there when Maddie and Angeline arrived. But instead of playing games as they usually did before class started, they were all huddled in silence at the edge of the clearing. Maddie quickly saw why.

The pine-slab benches that had been so lovingly built for their church had been turned over and thrown haphazardly around the clearing. Most were destroyed. It looked like somebody had taken an ax and chopped them into kindling wood. Even the crate that had been their pulpit was reduced to splinters.

"Who would've done this?" Angeline stared at the destruction in horror.

Maddie shook her head, unable to speak.

"It was them bluecoats," one of the older boys said. "They hates us. I heared 'em say the coloreds on this island live better'n they do, and it's gotta stop."

One of the little girls started to cry. Maddie scooped her up and tried to soothe her.

Angeline said, "We better send ever'body home till we can talk to Papa."

Titus couldn't believe it when Maddie and Angeline told him. Ella was frightened. "We hoped for too much," she said. "There's no Promised Land for slaves this side'a the grave."

"We ain't slaves!" Titus's eyes flashed with fury. "I'm goin' up to that army camp and tell the cap'n what's been done. We got a right to our church and school."

"No, Titus." Ella tried to grab his arm as he strode from the tent, but he shook her off.

"Papa!" Maddie called after him. She was scared. *Nobody* ever went in demanding to see the captain. He was the big man! And she had never seen Papa so mad. What if he hit somebody? Slave or not, she knew the soldiers wouldn't sit still for him striking a white man.

Titus was gone a long time. When he came back, he looked more tired than angry. "Cap'n don't believe soldiers did it," he said. "He sez we gotta prove it was soldiers 'fore he kin do anythin'."

"Then what?" Ella said bitterly. "Will he punish one'a his own for wreckin' a slave church?"

Titus's mouth tightened. "Sez he will, if it was soldiers that done it. And he sez they'll make us new benches."

A few days later, Maddie arrived at school to find the new benches lined up in front of a sturdy pine pulpit. After that, she often saw Sergeant Taylor standing at the edge of the clearing watching the lessons. Then one morning he arrived with several soldiers. Each of the soldiers carried a stack of wooden squares that had been neatly cut and sanded.

"Thought your pupils could use somethin' to write on," the sergeant said to Maddie as the soldiers distributed the squares.

The students were smiling and exclaiming over their makeshift slates. "This is real thoughtful of you," Maddie said to the sergeant.

"It's nothin' much," he said gruffly, already turning to leave.

Several days later Maddie received another pleasant surprise. When she and Angeline arrived for class, she saw a new pupil seated near the front, between Martha and a little boy named Joe. It was Zebedee.

He grinned at her and she grinned back. Martha looked pleased too. Maddie wondered if this was why the old woman had come to school in the first place.

When Titus and Royall weren't working on the fort,

they were searching the banks of the island for pieces of lumber that had washed ashore. Titus was worried about his family making it through the winter with only thin canvas to protect them from the fierce ocean winds.

Often Maddie and Zebedee would join them in the search. But lumber was scarce. A few of the families had cut logs to build themselves rough little cabins, but most of the residents would make do with fortified tents and lean-tos.

Just as summer had come early to Roanoke Island this year, so did autumn. By late September, the mornings were already crisp and cool. Maddie felt the chill when she carried water from the well.

One morning, Maddie met Titus as she was coming back with the water. He was standing at the opening to the tent, looking up at the rose- and gold-streaked sky.

"Look at that, daughter," he said softly. "Did you ever see such a sight?"

Maddie followed his gaze to the east, where the sky was alive with hundreds of beating wings. The birds were white, with black-tipped wings.

She came over to stand with Titus. He placed an arm around her shoulder. "What are they, Papa?"

"Snow geese." Royall had come out of his tent. He walked over to join them. "Comes down from Canada this time ever' year. Spends the winter over on Pea Island."

"Snow geese," Maddie repeated. "That's a beautiful name."

"Suits 'em," Titus said.

"Think how much'a the world they see," Maddie said. She didn't know where this place called Canada was, but it must be far away from North Carolina. "Wouldn't it be nice to fly anywhere you wanted to?"

"It shorely would be," Titus agreed. "Many's a day I envied the birds, with the whole sky their home."

They stood and watched the snow geese until the last one disappeared from sight.

Eighteen

"Whoever heard'a spendin' Christmas in a smelly old tent?" Angeline grumbled as she stitched on a shirt for Pride.

"We're havin' a fine meal Christmas Day," Maddie consoled her, "what with the game Papa and Royall's brought in, and the good things from Mama's garden. And we'll have fruit pies and biscuits—maybe even a cake."

"All you think about's your stomach," Angeline muttered. She frowned at the crooked line of stitches she'd made. "Papa said we'd have a real house, and we're no closer than we were last spring."

"Papa says the fort and docks are nearly done. Then he and Royall can start on the houses."

The mention of houses—in the plural—cheered Angeline. It was her dearest wish to marry Royall and be the mistress of her own house. But Mama and Papa, while giving Angeline and Royall their blessing to court, stubbornly refused to let them marry until summer.

In preparation for Christmas, Titus and Royall had made long tables of split pine logs and set them up outside the Henrys' tent. A special meal was planned, along with dancing and fiddle music and singing—just like on the plantation. But this year, Titus reminded them, there would be no master or mistress to tell them how to feast or when to feel grateful. Yessir, he said, this year they surely did have something to celebrate.

As Christmas Day drew near, Ella became quiet.

"She's worryin' about the Mistress," Angeline told Maddie as they cracked pecans for a pie. "She still can't rest easy about runnin' off and leavin' her."

"Where you reckon Mistress is now?" Maddie wondered.

"Back at River Bend—'less the Yankees've come. Could be burned to the ground by now."

Maddie didn't like to think of that happening to anybody, even the Mistress. She couldn't imagine men like Sergeant Taylor leaving people without a home. But there were others—like the ones who'd wrecked the church—who might burn folks out without a thought.

On the day before Christmas, Martha and some of the other women brought their pots to Ella's tent. They would spend the day fixing tomorrow's dinner, while the men played their fiddles and drums, kept the fires going, and talked about other Christmases they remembered.

The work and reminiscences were in full swing when soldiers arrived with a load of crates. "Christmas presents for everybody," Sergeant Taylor told them.

They all received clothes and shoes, and Maddie got a pretty cape of soft gray wool. She was slipping the cape around her shoulders when the sergeant called her name again.

"Come on," he said when she hesitated. "There's one more present here. Just the thing for the camp's teacher."

The sergeant was taking something out of one of the crates.

"It's a book," Angeline whispered, "like the ones in Master's library! Go on, Maddie, take it."

The sergeant placed the volume in Maddie's hands. It

was bound in soft green leather, with a design of gold leaves and flowers along its spine. And it *was* as beautiful as any of the Master's books.

Maddie stroked the cover. Was it possible that this was really hers?

"It's a book'a poems by a man named Walt Whitman," the sergeant said. "It's called *Leaves of Grass.*"

"What's a poem?" Angeline asked.

"A rhyme," he said. "Sort of a song without music."

Maddie looked up at Sergeant Taylor. He was smiling at her. "Thank you," she said softly. She clutched the book of poems to her chest.

That night the contraband camp had its party. They drank elderberry wine and danced to fiddle music.

Even Brother Earl danced, swinging first Maddie, then Angeline, around the clearing. Titus danced with Ella. Royall danced with Angeline. And as they danced, they clapped their hands and sang.

> *Juba this and Juba that.*
> *Juba killed a yeller cat.*
> *Juba this and Juba that.*
> *Hold your partner where you's at.*

Zebedee firmly refused when Maddie tried to get him to do the dance called "Cuttin' the Pigeon Wing." But Maddie didn't mind, because this was the best Christmas ever. She was free. She had a book of her own. Somehow, they meant the same thing to her.

Even though the party lasted into the night, everybody was up early the next morning. The women had cooking to do, the men wood to bring in, the children presents to admire.

Maddie was the first of her family to wake. "Christmas

gift," she said to Angeline, who still slept beside her. "Christmas gift," she called to the others.

"Christmas gift," Angeline murmured groggily.

"Too late," Maddie cried. "I said it first—so you have to give me a gift!"

It wasn't until evening that Maddie had time to look at her book properly, one page at a time. Ella was singing as she rocked Pride to sleep. Everybody else was sitting quietly, full and content.

"Read to us from your new book," Titus said.

Maddie began to read from the book that lay open in her lap.

Afoot and light-hearted I take to the open road,
Healthy, free, the world before me,
The long brown path before me leading wherever I choose.

Maddie read on, sometimes stumbling over a difficult word. She didn't understand everything she read, but she felt the strength and excitement of Mr. Whitman's message.

Allons! we must not stop here,
However sweet these laid-up stores, however convenient this
*   dwelling we cannot remain here,*
However shelter'd this port and however calm these waters we
*   must not anchor here,*
However welcome the hospitality that surrounds us we are
*   permitted to receive it but a little while.*

Allons! the inducements will be greater,
We will sail pathless and wild seas,
We will go where winds blow, waves dash, and the Yankee
*   clipper speeds by under full sail.*

When Maddie finally closed the book for the night, no one spoke. She thought they had all fallen asleep.

Then Titus stirred. "Them's powerful words, daughter," he said. "I think this Whitman feller understands about wantin' to be free. You kin read us this again sometime."

"There's lots of poems in the book, Papa."

"Then we'll hear them all," Titus said. "But I think I'll still favor this one."

Nineteen

Shortly after the beginning of the new year, Sergeant Taylor told the contrabands to come to the army camp. His captain had something to tell them.

Forever after, Maddie would smile when she remembered that day. Wasn't it just like her to cause trouble on one of the most important days of their lives?

There were soldiers hanging around the camp watching the contrabands arrive. But Maddie was more interested in the three horses tethered at the headquarters building. She poked Zebedee in the ribs and pointed to the horses. He grinned his understanding.

"A white, a black, and a brown," she whispered. "I can get some of each color. Won't old Sula just hate it?"

Sula Jackson was a new girl in the camp. She had brought with her two objects that were greatly coveted by Maddie and the other girls—a bracelet and a ring made of braided horsehair. Now they all wanted horsehair jewelry. But horses were scarce on the island, and nobody had found the courage to enter the army stables and pluck the hairs they needed. So Sula had been waving her hand around every chance she got, lording it over them something terrible.

While the other contrabands gathered at the headquarters building to listen to the captain, Maddie and Zebedee sidled over to where the horses were tied. Maddie positioned herself behind the brown horse, and Zeb headed for the white.

The captain was talking. Loud voices suddenly erupted. But Maddie was too preoccupied to notice. She reached for the brown horse's tail and grasped a few coarse hairs. Zebedee grabbed the white horse's tail. At the same moment, they yanked.

The horses kicked in unison, then reared. They pulled loose from their tethers and loped into the crowd. People screamed, swore, and ran for safety. Soldiers sprinted after the runaway animals. The sergeant turned to look at Maddie and Zebedee, who were still standing beside the remaining horse.

The captain looked angry. He started toward Maddie and Zeb, followed by Sergeant Taylor. Titus and Ella hurried after them.

"What did you do to those horses?" the captain demanded when he reached Maddie and Zebedee. The fury in his voice terrified Maddie.

The sergeant looked more puzzled than angry. When he saw the long hairs trailing from Maddie's and Zebedee's fingers, he shot them a questioning look.

"They didn't mean no harm—" Titus said quickly, but the captain cut him off.

"Answer me!" he barked at Maddie and Zeb. "Were you tryin' to steal those horses?"

Maddie tried to speak, but no sound came out.

"Looks like they just got too close and spooked the horses," the sergeant said. His calm reassured Maddie a little, but she was shaking all over.

"Don't we do enough for these people without them stealing us blind?" the captain said. Still glaring at Maddie and Zebedee, he said, "Sergeant, issue a notice. Any person found near our horses, or any other government property, will be taken to the guardhouse and whipped."

The captain stalked off.

Titus gripped Maddie's shoulders. "What was you thinkin' of?" He spoke quietly, but his voice was like flint.

"We only wanted a few hairs from their tails," Maddie whispered.

"Sweet Jesus," Ella muttered. "Always doin' 'fore she thinks."

"You know what trouble you coulda caused?" Titus demanded.

"I'm sorry, Papa—"

"Go back to the tent and stay there. You too, Zebedee."

The sergeant was staring at Maddie, but he was smiling a little. "Don't be too hard on 'em for a little mischief," he said. "This is a great day for them too."

Even in her misery, Maddie wondered what the sergeant meant. Why was this a great day?

"President Lincoln's freed the slaves," Angeline told her. "On the first day of the new year, he issued the"— she faltered and looked to Sergeant Taylor for help— "what's it called?"

"The Emancipation Proclamation. Means all people held as slaves in the Confederate states are free."

Zebedee whooped. "You hear that, Maddie? We's free!"

Maddie looked to Titus. She was relieved to see that he was smiling now. "Are we, Papa? Are we free?"

"Some of us are," he said, trying to look stern again. "The ones not up to mischief."

Ella was still frowning at her. "Whatever comes over you, Maddie?"

119

"Does this mean the war's over?" Zebedee asked the sergeant.

" 'Fraid not, son. The president's proclamation says the slaves are free, but it's gonna take the North winnin' the war to enforce it. Just be glad you're on Roanoke Island. The rest of the slaves out there are still in bondage, no matter what that piece'a paper says."

Winter was finally over, and Maddie and her family were beginning their second spring on Roanoke Island. The fort and docks were finished, but this was a mixed blessing. The men would finally have time to build their houses; but now that the army work was done, they wouldn't be paid.

"We put aside near ever' cent we made," Titus reassured Ella. "We'll get by."

"Some months you weren't paid at all," Ella said. "They still owe us."

"Some'a the men are goin' to the cap'n about it."

Ella shook her head. "They've gone to the cap'n before," she said, "and we're still waitin'."

A few days later she said to Titus, "Some'a the women work at the army camp, doin' cookin' and cleanin'. Maybe they'll take me on."

"Don't want my wife goin' to that camp," Titus said. "No tellin' what some'a them soldiers might do."

"You got your heart set on buyin' a farm, don't you?" Ella insisted. "We'll need a lot more money than what we got."

"We'll get our farm without you workin' for the army."

"Maybe so, but I'm gonna bring it up to Sergeant Taylor next time I see him."

She saw the sergeant a week later.

"We've already got all the help we need," he told her. "But maybe I can find something for you," he added, when he saw her disappointment.

The next day he told Ella to report to the garrison. She would wash and iron clothes for the soldiers. Ella set off with some trepidation, leaving Angeline in charge at home.

Soon after, the contrabands were called again to the army camp. This time Maddie stayed close to Ella and Titus.

"We just got word the government's setting up a permanent community for freed slaves here on the island," the captain told them. "The unoccupied land to the north will be divided into one-acre lots. A lot will be assigned to each family."

"You mean, you're givin' us the land?" somebody in the crowd called out.

"That's what I've been told to do," the captain said. But Maddie thought he didn't sound happy about it. "The land's been confiscated from its owners. The president's giving it to you in repayment for your loyalty to the Union."

A buzz of excitement spread through the crowd. They all began to ask questions at once. When would the land be theirs? Where would they get supplies to build houses?

"Military surveyors will be here soon to divide up the land," the captain told them. "They'll clear the trees and put in the streets for you, but you'll be expected to build your own houses. We'll see you get the tools you need."

"It's not what I had in mind," Titus said over supper that night, "but the land would be ours."

"We can grow all the vegetables we need on an acre, and keep a cow and chickens besides," Ella said eagerly. She had dreaded another move to a strange place.

"We can stay here with all our friends," Angeline said, thinking that she and Royall could have a good life on their acre, surrounded by people they knew and loved.

"With the war still on, we don't have much say in the matter, anyhow," Titus said. "We're safe here."

"What about Zebedee?" Maddie asked suddenly. "Will he get an acre too?"

"Zebedee's just a boy," Ella said. "He'll go on livin' with Doc and Martha."

"But he wants his own house," Maddie protested. "Doc and Martha aren't family."

"They *are* a mite old to be carin' for a boy like Zeb," Titus said. "Ella, why cain't he come live with us? He's here all the time, anyhow."

Ella hesitated. "What about Doc and Martha? They'll need Zebedee to help build their house."

"He can still help," Titus said. "Royall and me will, too."

"Zeb would pay his way," Maddie said. "He's a hard worker."

"He is," Titus agreed. "And the boy needs a home, Ella. A fam'ly he kin call his own."

"Looks like it's settled then," Ella said. "You can ask him if you want, Titus."

"I think he might cotton to the idea more if it came from Maddie." He smiled at his younger daughter. "Let's you and me go talk to Doc and Martha."

Zebedee resisted the idea at first, but his objections sounded hollow to Maddie. She was pretty sure he was relieved to have the worry of building a house taken off his shoulders.

The surveying team came in June. They made quick work of plotting the land and clearing it for building. Almost every day Maddie and Zebedee walked to where the work was being done, and watched with wonder as broad, straight streets began to appear.

Titus and Royall requested adjoining lots. As soon as their land was assigned, they began to cut logs and haul them to the sites. They would build Titus's house first, then Doc and Martha's. When those were finished, they would work on Royall's house.

Everybody except Pride was involved in building the house. While the men cut logs, notched their ends, and rolled them into place to form the walls, Ella, Angeline, and Maddie filled buckets with clay, which they daubed into the cracks.

Titus, Royall, and Zebedee made the roof by splitting the logs into flat planks and securing them with the precious nails supplied by the army. They cut holes in the walls for doors and windows. Then they cut planks to make doors and shutters.

On the day the house was finished, they all stood looking at it without saying a word. It was a lot bigger and sturdier than the cabins Maddie remembered from slave row. There was a main room downstairs, where they would live and cook, with separate rooms for storing food and for Ella and Titus to sleep. In the loft were two rooms—one for Angeline and Maddie, the other for Zebedee. When Pride was a little older, he would move out of Ella and Titus's room and share Zeb's.

"What a fine house you've built me," Ella said to Titus. "These walls will keep out the cold this winter."

His eyes glowed with pride. "Later on, we can lay a floor downstairs. Someday I'll put real glass in them windows for you, Ella."

"Glass windows couldn't make me happier than I am this minute," Ella said.

"Soon you'll have a room to yourself," Angeline told Maddie. "In two months I'll be fifteen. After we're married, I'll be livin' in Royall's house."

Maddie felt an ache of loneliness when she thought of Angeline leaving. But she tried to tell herself that living right next door was nearly as good as sharing a room with Angeline.

"Hasn't been so bad in this old tent," Maddie said on their last night there.

"I sure won't miss it," Angeline said. "Still smells like a wet hound."

Maddie breathed in and, sure enough, smelled the distinct odor of wet animal. She began to giggle, then Angeline got started. And before long they were all laughing so hard, they were holding their bellies and gasping for air. Even Ella.

So Mama was finally happy, Maddie thought. Maybe she felt safe at last. Maybe now she could stop fretting about running off from the Mistress.

Ella noticed Maddie watching her, and she stopped laughing. She smiled at Maddie, the kind of gentle smile that Maddie had always longed for from Mama. Did that mean that Mama had forgiven her for being so different from Angeline and herself?

All of a sudden Maddie realized how hard she and Papa had made life for Ella. All Ella had ever wanted was a safe life on the plantation, with her family growing up well fed and strong. But Papa's dreams had meant an end to that safety. And Maddie was like Papa, not mindful enough of rules and the consequences of breaking them. How she must have frightened Mama.

For the first time in her life, Maddie felt that she understood Mama. And her heart softened, allowing her to forgive Ella and accept whatever love her mama could give. Was she finally beginning to grow up, as Mama had wanted? Maddie thought so. Suddenly she felt older— older even than Angeline, who was walking around in a fog these days, her head filled with silly dreams of being Royall's wife.

Twenty

When Doc and Martha's house was finished, Titus and Royall began to build furniture: a sturdy pine bed for Titus and Ella, and a table and chairs that would seat them all for meals. Then they put up shelves in the storage room for food.

While the men built the furniture, Ella, Angeline, and Maddie filled new mattresses with pine needles and made curtains from a bolt of white muslin that had come from the North. Ella planted her vegetable garden at the rear of the house, and Titus brought home chickens, a hog, and a cow from the settlement on the southern end of the island.

One morning Maddie was helping Ella in the garden, while Angeline and Pride milked the cow. Next door, Titus, Royall, and Zebedee were putting up the walls of Royall's house.

"Angeline and Royall's house is bigger'n ours," Maddie said.

"They'll need room for the children they'll have." Ella shaded her eyes with her hand as she looked toward Royall's lot. "Your sister's mighty lucky to be startin' her married life with such a fine house."

Maddie grunted. "She's still too young to be jumpin' the broom."

Ella's gaze slipped from the men to Maddie. "Someday you'll meet a man you wanta marry, daughter. Then you'll understand why Angeline's impatient."

"I don't think so!" Maddie responded, so emphatically that Ella laughed.

"It'll happen," Ella assured her gently.

Maddie was washing breakfast dishes a few days later when Royall burst in looking for Titus. "The army's enlistin' colored men! When I heard, I run to Sergeant Taylor, and he sez it's the truth."

"We saw men gatherin' at the headquarters," Titus said. "Wondered what it was about."

"They's givin' us a chance to fight the people that done kept us slaves, and payin' us besides," Royall said. "You're signin' up, ain't you?"

"Cain't say I ever thought'a bein' a soldier," Titus said. "I'm a good bit older'n you, son. This here war's a fight for young men."

"But you ain't old," Royall protested. "Why, you fell trees and tote logs easy as me."

"Cain't have you shamin' me, now, kin I?" Titus said with a grin.

"Well, *I'm* joinin' up," Royall said. "I thought you'd be as glad to go as me."

"And what about me?" Angeline demanded. "We're to be married in a month's time, Royall Tate. Or did that slip your mind?"

" 'Course it didn't. But Angeline, they's treatin' us like any other man, not carin' about the color of our skin."

"And you can die like any other man," Angeline said angrily. "We've had enough troubles. It's time to settle down on our land and enjoy our freedom."

"But it's the land and the freedom I'm thinkin' about," Royall insisted. "If the South wins this here war, we won't have no land. We'll be slaves again."

"There's truth in what you say," Titus said before Angeline could speak. "We cain't 'spect the army to do all our fightin' for us."

"Why are men so quick to want'a fight?" Angeline said bitterly.

"You understand, don't you, wife?" Titus asked Ella.

"As good as I'm able." Ella sighed. "Angeline, women can't win when their men's pride is at stake."

"Pride!" Angeline spat out the word. "Whatta I care about pride? All I want's my man alive!" She ran outside.

Ella touched Royall's arm to keep him from following Angeline. "Leave her be," Ella said wearily. "She'll come to accept it if she has to."

Titus and Royall were admitted into the army along with a hundred other men from the island. Going into the third year of the war, the Union Army was looking a little less fine than it had in 1861. Uniforms were old, and those given to the freed-slave troops were the worst of the lot. But Maddie saw the delight in her papa's eyes when he put on the army coat and hat.

Titus and Royall received rifles with bayonets. They started drilling with the other troops every day. They learned how to march, how to avoid enemy fire, and how to load and fire and clean their weapons.

The white soldiers gathered to watch the new recruits train. Sometimes they laughed when the marchers got out of step. Sometimes they grumbled about slaves carrying guns. Maddie heard them and it made her angry. Her papa would be as good a soldier as any one of them!

"Royall sho' did take to bein' in the army," Titus said

the night before they were to leave the island. "He picks up that rifle like he's been doin' it ever' day of his life."

Maddie was putting away supper dishes while Angeline and Royall took a last walk together. No one had asked what she thought about the men going off to fight in the war. But if they had, she would have said she knew why they had to go. For the first time in her thirteen years, Maddie regretted that she was a girl. Because girls weren't allowed to fight. Not that she wanted to kill anybody, or be killed herself. But, like Papa and Royall, she believed they had a duty to fight for their freedom.

Maddie knew that Zebedee was suffering too, because he was too young to enlist. He had begged Titus to take him along, but Titus had told him that one man had to stay home to take care of the family. Zebedee had accepted Titus's decision. But he had looked at the uniforms with such longing, Maddie knew it was only a matter of time before he'd follow the other men into battle.

Angeline had accepted the temporary loss of Royall, and her delayed marriage, but nobody could force her to be happy about it. Maddie saw that her sister's eyes were red and swollen when she and Royall returned from their walk. Royall looked miserable.

"I don't want'a remember all these long faces," Titus remarked as he looked around the room at them. "Let me have some smiles to take with me."

Maddie came to sit beside her papa. She forced a smile. Ella tried. But Angeline just stared into the fire, tight-lipped and distant.

Titus stroked Maddie's head. "Know what I'd like my last night at home?" he asked. "I'd like to hear Maddie read that poem about the open road. Will you do that, daughter?"

Maddie took the book over to the fireplace where she could see. Titus had requested the poem so often, the book fell open to it.

Afoot and light-hearted I take to the open road,
Healthy, free, the world before me,
The long brown path before me leading wherever I choose.

When she had finished the long poem, Maddie closed the book, feeling mighty lonely. "I'll miss readin' to you, Papa."

"I 'spect you to go on readin' ever' night, just like I was here," Titus said. "Wherever I am, I'll hear you, Maddie. You just go on readin' and I'll hear."

Twenty-One

With many of the young men gone, the community changed. The house-building slowed down. Women and girls fished and trapped—and waited for their men to come back.

Maddie now had her own traps that she set out with Zebedee's. Fishing and trapping were serious business, since they meant food for the family. Everybody with a soldier in the family was given a ration of beef and a little fish, but it wasn't nearly enough to feed them all. Maddie's family shared their eggs, the milk from their cow, and the vegetables from Ella's garden with Doc and Martha and some of the other old people in the camp.

Maddie's school was still operating. Maddie and her students had moved into the one-room cabin of a single man who had joined the army. Zebedee made benches and a table. Now, on rainy days, they stayed snug and dry while they had their lessons. Runaways were still coming to the island, and Maddie had a constant flow of new children who were eager to learn to read and write.

Each evening Ella returned from the garrison with news of the war. Sometimes there was a short letter from Royall, assuring them that he and Titus were well and missing them all. But as the weeks passed, the letters became more infrequent, until they finally stopped coming altogether. It must be hard to find time to write in the middle of a war, Maddie insisted to Ella and Angeline. And they agreed quickly, unwilling to think about any other possibilities.

As usual, summer on Roanoke Island was especially hot and miserable. By late August, the hospital was filled with old people and children stricken by summer fevers and the bloody flux, a devastating illness that left many cradles empty. After school each day, Maddie and Angeline went to help at the hospital.

Sister Melba was too busy to pay them much mind except when she was barking out orders to them. But Maddie saw how gently the woman cared for her patients, using some of the same remedies as Aunt Lucy.

One day, Sister Melba noticed Maddie watching her. "You know how to fix a horehound plaster?" she asked. "Come here, I'll show you."

After that, Sister Melba often asked for Maddie's help when she was making a poultice or brewing a healing tea. Aunt Lucy would be proud, Maddie thought.

" 'Magine I'll die alone someday," Angeline said one evening as she was helping Ella and Maddie fix supper. She spoke softly, but there was such melodrama in her voice, Maddie laughed.

"You can think it's funny," Angeline said crossly. "Your beau's still here with you."

"My what?" Maddie nearly dropped the plates she was holding.

"Zebedee. Your beau."

"Zebedee's not my beau."

"Maddie's too young for courtin'," Ella agreed.

"She's thirteen, same age I was when I met Royall," Angeline said. "And they're together all the time."

Ella looked worried.

"But it's not like that," Maddie insisted. "Zeb's like a brother." She scowled at Angeline. "Don't go makin' up somethin' that's not there—just 'cause you're dyin' to get married."

Ella looked relieved. "There'll be time enough later for that, Angeline. Don't be rushin' your sister."

After that, however, Maddie felt Ella watching her when she was with Zebedee. Maddie was astounded that anybody would think of her and Zebedee as sweethearts. Because she surely couldn't!

Ella and Angeline had accepted Zebedee into their home without ever making him a part of the family. But two things happened that summer to change their feelings toward him.

One evening after supper they were sitting outside, trying to find relief from the heat.

"Royall's house sho' do look lonesome settin' there," Zebedee said.

"He'll finish it when they get back," Ella said.

"Why wait till then?" Zebedee asked. "They done got some'a the walls up. I could cut the rest of the logs, if Maddie and Angeline was a mind to help."

Angeline came alive. "Could you really, Zeb?"

"Ain't much to it now."

"Logs are too heavy for the girls to lift," Ella said.

"Not if we all work together," Angeline said. "Will you help, Maddie?"

Seeing the hope on Angeline's face, Maddie knew she couldn't say no. "I'll help."

"Is it all right, Miz Ella?" Zebedee asked. "We'll make time for our other work."

Ella looked from Zebedee's solemn face to Angeline's glowing one. "How can I say no? But you watch after my girls, Zebedee."

"Yes'm. I'll make sure nothin' happens to 'em."

They worked on the house every day after that. Progress was slow, but finally they had the walls in place and the roof on. Zebedee cut the doors and windows where Angeline directed.

After that, Maddie noticed that nothing was too good for Zeb, as far as her sister was concerned. He got the biggest helpings at supper, and the first slice of a just-made pie. Angeline gave him all the care and affection she had previously reserved for her family and Royall.

A few days later, Zebedee went fishing. It started to rain. By the time the boy came home, he was soaked to the skin.

"You get out of them clothes," Ella ordered. "Here's a dry shirt."

Before he could object, she was peeling the wet shirt off him. Maddie took no notice until Zebedee started to protest.

"No'm, I'm fine the way I am. My shirt ain't that wet—"

"Zebedee, will you stop your hollerin'?" Ella pulled his shirt off.

Maddie wasn't prepared for the sight of Zebedee's back, for the deep, ugly scars etched into his skin.

"Lord'a mercy," Ella whispered. "Child, what did they do to you?"

She touched his back. Zeb jerked away and stared at the floor.

"Your master did this?" Ella asked softly.

"Yes'm," Zebedee mumbled.

"Never seen a child whipped like this." Ella's hand lit on his shoulder, and he didn't pull away. "Why, Zeb?"

"Stole some bacon from the smokehouse when my mama was sick." He looked up at Ella defiantly. "We never got enough to eat, and it didn't hardly seem right for her to die hungry. But he caught me 'fore I could get back to the cabin. Got sick, myself, from the whoopin'. Didn't know day from night for four days. Weren't there for my mama when she died, or to see her buried."

Maddie's eyes met Ella's.

"Guess I'll be cleanin' these fish," Zebedee said. He reached for the dry shirt in Ella's hand and draped it over his shoulders.

When he was gone, Ella sank into a chair. "Titus was right to go," she said, more to herself than to Maddie. "If a master can do that to a child, we can't ever go back to slavery—no matter what."

"He was just tryin' to help his mama," Maddie said. "What he did wasn't so bad, even if he was stealin'."

"Bad? Why, Maddie, what he did was an act of love. We got us a fine young man in our family now," she added softly. "I won't ever question his right to be here again."

Twenty-Two

Summer drifted slowly into fall, and still there was no word from Titus and Royall. And no army pay, either. Many of the wives had complained bitterly to the captain that their husbands were risking their lives for less than the white soldiers were paid, and the army was withholding even that. The captain had promised to look into it. Meanwhile, the four dollars a month that Ella made washing and ironing was the only money coming in.

Maddie and Zebedee gathered crab apples, picked the last of the peas, dug up potatoes, and gathered the corn. By late September, the storeroom was filled with food, as well as the dried herbs and roots that Sister Melba was teaching Maddie to use.

One day in October, Maddie and Zebedee were walking home from school when they saw Sergeant Taylor.

"Any news from Papa and Royall?" Maddie asked, as she always did.

"Not yet. But I have some other news. There's a teacher comin' to the island."

"A real teacher?"

The sergeant nodded. "A lady named Miss Elizabeth James, from up North. The American Missionary Society's sendin' her." His gray eyes twinkled. "They don't know we already have a school and a teacher."

Maddie digested the news of the teacher slowly. She

had always wanted to go to school, and be taught by a real teacher. But she also loved *being* the teacher, and having the little ones look to her for help. Once Miss James came, all that would end.

"Will she bring books?" Maddie asked.

"Don't think they'd send her here without books."

That settled it. New books were more important to Maddie than her role of teacher. She smiled at the sergeant. "When'll she get here?"

"Any day now."

Within a week, the ship arrived bringing Miss James and a large number of trunks and crates. Maddie was there when the soldiers brought her baggage to the small house where Miss James would live. And then Maddie saw the teacher herself.

She was tall and slender, with soft brown hair pulled into a knot at the nape of her neck. Maddie thought she had never seen a prettier woman. Miss James didn't have Mistress McCartha's golden angel's hair, but her eyes were bright and curious, and her lips curved into a generous smile.

Two days after Miss James's arrival, word spread that children between the ages of five and sixteen were invited to attend school the next morning.

"I don't need no white woman's school," Zebedee assured Maddie. "I learn plenty good from you."

"But she's a real teacher," Maddie said. She was grateful for his loyalty, but determined to have the best for him. "You'll learn more from her, and so will I."

The next morning they both set off for the one-room cabin that would be their new school. When they got there, Maddie saw a flock of new students—as well as many of her own. Miss James stood at the door and smiled at each student who filed into the cabin. "Welcome to the Roanoke Island School," she said. "Please come in and take your seats."

Their seats turned out to be nothing more than over-turned crates, the customary furnishings on the island. Maddie hurried to the front, pulling a resistant Zebedee by the hand, and captured two prized seats in front of the teacher's desk.

That's when she saw the stacks of books that covered the desk and the floor nearby. She nudged Zebedee and pointed to the books. Miss James noticed Maddie's inter-est in the books and gave her an even warmer smile. Right then and there Maddie decided that she loved this beautiful teacher, and she was going to do everything she could to be like her.

"My name is Miss James," the woman said when all the children were seated. "I'll write my name on the board for you."

Behind the teacher's desk was a big, square board that looked like a piece of slate rock to Maddie. She watched in wonderment as the teacher took a small white stick and printed her name on the board.

"If anyone here knows how to read, will you raise your hand?" Miss James said. She looked surprised when more than half the students raised their hands.

Miss James handed a book to a little girl in the front row. "Open it anywhere and read a passage aloud, please."

" 'Columbus sought a way to reach the riches of the Orient. Instead, he found a New World.' "

"Very good," Miss James said. She passed the book to a boy in the second row. "Why don't you try it?"

" 'By 1700, there were more than a quarter of a million

colonists in the New World,' " the boy read. " 'By 1765, their numbers had reached nearly two million.' "

Miss James walked around the room with the book, stopping at desk after desk to ask the children to read. Finally she returned to the front, a puzzled expression on her face. "I'm amazed—and very pleased—to see that so many of you can read. But I thought it was against the law to teach slave children to read and write."

"We didn't know how till we come to the island," somebody called from the back of the room.

"Someone here taught you?" Miss James asked.

"Maddie did."

"And she taught us to write too."

"And do sums," Zebedee added.

"Who is Maddie?" the teacher asked.

"This is her." Zebedee placed a hand on Maddie's arm. "This here's our teacher."

Miss James walked over to Maddie. "How did you learn to read and write and do sums, Maddie?"

"My mama taught me." Maddie felt shy now that the beautiful teacher was standing so close and speaking to her directly. "Ever' night after we came back from the Big House, she'd give my sister and me lessons to do."

"And you started a school when you came to the island?"

"Yes'm, Miz James. But I know you're the teacher now," she added hastily. "And I'm happy you're here. There's so much I want to learn." Her eyes strayed to the stack of books. "And I wanta read as many books as I can."

"And read them you shall," Miss James said gently. "But, you know, Maddie, there are too many children here for me to teach all at once. It might be a good idea for you to keep helping the beginners with their letters. How would you like to be both pupil and teacher?"

Maddie couldn't believe she had heard correctly. It seemed too good to be true. Of course she would help Miss James!

"Will you help me, Maddie?"

"Yes, ma'am," Maddie said gravely. "Any way I can."

From that morning on, Maddie's life fell into yet another pattern. While Miss James taught one group their numbers, Maddie instructed another class in reading. Then Maddie joined everyone for lessons in geography and history.

Miss James read to them from the Bible and taught them hymns they had never heard before. She talked about responsibility and being ready to accept their freedom once the war was over.

"You children are lucky," she said one morning toward the end of class. "Here on the island you can learn skills that will help you take your place in a free society. The rest of the country is locked in a bitter war, but you and your families are safe. Make use of the opportunities you've been given. And someday you'll be able to help your brothers and sisters obtain their rightful places in society."

Maddie thought about the teacher's words often— especially the part about helping her brothers and sisters. After the war, that was what she would do. She would study hard, learn everything Miss James could teach her, and then she'd go back to River Bend. She would find Elsie and Louisa and her other friends on slave row, and teach them to read and write.

But it wasn't only the children who wanted to learn. Maddie remembered the look of pride on Martha's face the day she printed her name for the first time. Older people wanted learning, too, and somebody should teach them.

Maddie was stacking books one day after class when she decided to talk to Miss James about it. She still felt shy around the teacher, but Miss James was so kind, Maddie was no longer afraid to talk to her.

"Miz James, there's somethin' I've been thinkin' about."

"What's that, Maddie?" The teacher looked up from her writing.

"It's the old folks. Some of 'em wanta learn just like the children. I was teachin' 'em 'fore you came, and they caught on fast."

"So you think there should be a school for the grown-ups?"

"Yes, ma'am, I surely do." Maddie hesitated. "Don't the older folks need to learn about livin' in a free society too?"

Miss James studied Maddie's earnest face for a moment. Then she said, "Indeed, they do, Maddie Henry. Your idea's a good one. I'll visit some of the families and see how many are interested. But this will mean a lot of extra work. Are you willing to help me again?"

Maddie's smile was all the answer Miss James needed.

Maddie expected Ella to object to all the time she was spending with the school, but Ella surprised her.

"You go on helpin' Miz James," Ella said. "Your papa would like that."

Whenever Ella mentioned Titus, her voice grew soft and wistful. Day after day they waited, and still there was no word from the men. But Maddie knew that they would come back. They had to.

Twenty-Three

It was a week before Christmas. Maddie was sitting at the table cutting wicks for the candles Ella was making. Ella was stirring a pot of tallow over the fire, and Zebedee was mending his traps.

When the door opened, and Maddie felt the rush of cold air, she didn't even look up from her work. It was time for Angeline to come back from the hospital, to watch Pride while Ella and Zebedee took clean laundry to the army camp. Maddie expected to hear Ella greet her older daughter and ask how her morning had gone.

Instead, she heard Ella say, "Angeline! What's wrong?"

Maddie looked up to see Angeline slumped against the door.

Ella let go of the stirring spoon and took a step toward Angeline. "Daughter, what's happened? Are you hurt?"

"I'm all right," Angeline whispered. She tried to smile but began to weep instead. "Mama, it's Royall. They brought him to the hospital this mornin'."

Ella's expression grew fearful. "Is he—"

"He was shot in the leg. He may never walk again, Mama, but he's alive!"

"And your papa?"

"He was well when Royall saw him a few weeks ago."

Ella sagged with relief, then revived quickly and led

Angeline to a chair by the fire. "Maddie, get your sister a cup of tea. And some for the rest of us too. The soldiers' laundry can wait."

Maddie brought the tea, and they listened while Angeline told her story.

"Two soldiers came in carryin' a man on a stretcher. I never dreamed it was Royall. The uniform was caked with blood . . ." Angeline was shivering, even though the tea and the fire should have warmed her. Ella brought a shawl and draped it around her shoulders.

"When I saw it was him, I was so scared," Angeline went on. "He looked like he was dead. But then he opened his eyes. I said his name, and he smiled at me 'fore he passed out."

"Where was he when he got hit?" Ella asked. "Where's your papa?"

"Somewhere in Virginia. Royall left Papa in Virginia."

"So far away," Ella murmured.

"An army surgeon took the bullet outta Royall's leg, said the bone was shattered, that he'd most likely lose the leg."

Ella squeezed Angeline's hand.

"I don't care about the leg, Mama," Angeline said fiercely. "All I want is Royall here—alive! Sister Melba says the leg's healin', that he probably won't lose it. But it may never support him again."

"How'd he get back here?" Maddie asked.

"Union soldiers comin' to North Carolina took him as far as New Bern. They said rebels wouldn't even bother to take a colored soldier prisoner—they'd shoot him dead on the spot if they caught him. Some other soldiers at New Bern brought him on to the island." Angeline

143

smiled. "He says he must'a told 'em a hundred times he wouldn't stop till he got here, even if he had to crawl and swim."

"Can we see him?" Maddie asked.

"Not just yet," Angeline said. "He's too weak to talk. I'm stayin' at the hospital with him."

"Not day and night, surely," Ella said, then stopped. She saw the stubborn set of Angeline's mouth. "All right, then, but go change your dress—you're covered with blood. I'll fix you food to take."

" 'Fore long, I can take Royall's place," Zebedee said as he turned back to his traps.

"I'll hear no more of that," Ella snapped. "Hasn't this family given enough?"

Two days later Maddie and Zebedee went to the hospital to visit Royall. Chills and fevers were epidemic this year, so most of the mattresses were filled.

Royall's face was gaunt and drawn with pain. But he was alert. "If it ain't little Maddie," he said in a weak voice. "And Zebedee." He squinted at the boy. "Looks like life with the Henrys is good for you, boy. You done put on weight."

"Royall, I'm so glad you're home, I don't even mind you marryin' Angeline," Maddie said.

"That's good to hear," Royall said, " 'cause I plan to marry that girl just as soon as I'm on two legs again. If she'll still have me."

Christmas Day arrived. Ella fixed her usual big dinner, even though Titus wasn't there and Royall was still in the hospital. Doc and Martha spent the day with them. Angeline stayed long enough to eat and then rushed off to be with Royall. It didn't seem like Christmas to Maddie. Not with Papa gone.

* * *

Royall came home a few days after Christmas. Once he was set up in Zebedee's room, Angeline went about nursing him with a vengeance. Nobody else could fix his tray or carry it up to him. Nobody else could bring him water or change his dressings. Ella allowed her to be with him all she wanted, while she and Maddie cared for the house and the rest of the family.

One night after Royall had been home about a week, Maddie woke up in the middle of the night. The sound of a deep, rasping cough echoed through the stillness of the house.

Wrapping a shawl around her, Maddie crept down the stairs and followed the sound to Ella's room.

Ella sat on the bed with Pride wrapped in a quilt in her arms. His small body jerked as he coughed.

"He's burnin' up," Ella said to Maddie. "And listen to him wheeze. I fixed a coltsfoot poultice, but it's not helpin'."

Maddie could see that fear had returned to Ella's eyes. Her mama looked small and helpless with her sick child in her arms.

"I'll brew some nettle tea," Maddie said. "Sister Melba uses it for fevers."

They forced Pride to drink the tea, but his fever kept rising. Maddie soaked a cloth in a horehound brew and put it on Pride's chest, as she had seen Sister Melba do. But still Pride coughed and wheezed, and his skin burned their fingers.

"It got bad so fast," Ella fretted. "He had a little cough today, but I barely noticed. I shoulda noticed! Maybe if I'd done somethin' then—"

"It's not your fault, Mama," Maddie said. "See if he'll drink more tea."

When Maddie had done everything she knew to do, and Pride was still no better, she said, "I'm goin' for Sister Melba."

In a short time, she returned with the healer. Sister Melba touched the boy's face, then pressed his neck with her fingertips. "Get my bag," she said to Maddie. "Take out two pinches of jimsonweed and start boilin' it."

At dawn, Angeline came to the door. She looked at her brother, then at Ella. "How bad is it?" she asked softly.

"Couldn't be much worse," Ella said. She stroked Pride's cheek. "We may lose him."

Maddie turned frightened eyes to Sister Melba.

The healer just shook her head. "I don't know," she said.

Pride hung on this way for two days. Maddie sent word to Miss James that she wouldn't be in school, and the teacher came by after class. When she saw that there was nothing she could do, she went home to pray.

Sister Melba came to the house several times a day. She listened to Maddie recite the remedies she had tried, then dug into her bag for new herbs.

Maddie was afraid to sleep. She feared that if she closed her eyes, Pride would be gone when she awoke.

There was no question of Ella sleeping. She refused to leave her boy in anybody else's care. "I gotta will him to fight," she said, when Maddie tried to force her to rest for just an hour.

On the morning of the third day, Maddie could stay awake no longer. Two hours before dawn, she slipped into sleep, even while she resisted it. As the sun came up, she awoke with a start.

The room was silent. The coughing had stopped. Ella

lay on the bed, her body wrapped protectively around the motionless bundle in her arms.

Maddie peered into her brother's still face. Gone were the gasps and whimpers. Her brother had lost the fight.

Maddie's weeping woke Ella. "Mama," Maddie said through her tears. "I should'a stayed awake—been here with you."

"Hush, Maddie," Ella said softly. "Hush, now. Our boy's better. Fever broke a while ago. He's sleepin' now."

"Then he's not—"

"No, Maddie. He's gonna be all right."

Twenty-Four

It was the coldest winter anybody on the Outer Banks could remember. Royall continued to improve in spite of it, but Pride was unable to regain his strength.

Angeline worked with Royall, exercising his leg as Sister Melba showed her and supporting him while he hobbled around the room on canes Zebedee had made him. Ella and Maddie cared for Pride. They kept him near the fire, wrapped in shawls and quilts. Ella made all his favorite foods, tempting him with spoon bread, apple pie, and strawberry preserves. But his cough and weakness remained.

Some evenings the fever returned. It was never as high as it had been those first days, but Ella grew terrified each time she felt the heat rising in her son's body. There were many nights during that long, dreary winter when neither Ella nor Maddie got any sleep.

When the spring of 1864 finally came, the community was exhausted, weary of body and spirit. There had been more illnesses on the island than ever before, and many of their numbers had lost the battle. Some of their men had died in the war. And other families, who had received no news, waited fearfully, hoping they wouldn't be the next to wear black armbands.

Royall and Ella received part of the army pay, with assurances that the rest would follow. Some of the families whose husbands and fathers were fighting in the war—or had died fighting it—were still waiting to see the first cent of pay.

After Pride was over the worst, Maddie went back to school. She was quieter now, and felt constantly tired from worry and lack of sleep. Miss James took one look at her and suggested that Maddie wait a while before returning to school. But Maddie refused to stay away.

By the end of April, Maddie's family was feeling some relief. Pride was still thin as a fence rail, but he coughed less, and some of his buoyancy had returned. Ella was letting him take short walks on sunny days.

Royall, too, was improving. He could manage the stairs by himself, leaning heavily on his canes, and walk around the yard without help. He had little feeling in his injured leg, and he couldn't bend it, so he walked with a limp. But Angeline was so proud of him, she glowed. He was standing on his own two feet, as the army surgeon and Sister Melba had thought he never would. There was nothing to stop them from getting married.

The wedding took place at the end of May, shortly before Angeline turned sixteen. Angeline and Royall didn't want to jump the broom and declare themselves married. They wanted a proper wedding service performed by Brother Earl.

Angeline wore a white muslin dress, which Ella had made for her. She carried a bouquet of pink primroses that Maddie had gathered. The halting steps of the groom, as he walked to the pulpit to meet his bride, brought tears to many eyes. Even Maddie felt her eyes mist, partly because she was happy, and partly because she knew that their lives were changing forever.

After the wedding, the community danced and sang

and drank elderberry wine. When the wedding couple stole away to their new home, no one but Ella and Maddie noticed.

Ella slipped an arm around her younger daughter's waist. Maddie knew her mama was thinking about Papa.

"He'll be happy when he comes home and finds 'em married," Maddie said.

Ella nodded, her face pensive. Then she smiled. "I think Zeb's had about enough of that pie. Why don't you drag him away from the food and make him dance with you?"

Royall set up a workshop in the back room of his house and started his own business. From sunrise to sunset he sat in the little room splitting wooden shingles to sell. Angeline worked in her garden, cared for her chickens and cow, and kept her house spotless.

"I'm truly blessed," she told Ella one day. "Mama, I want to live right here, just as we are, forever."

"What about babies?" Ella teased. "Only thing to be gained by losin' a daughter to marriage is the grandbabies she'll give you."

"There's time for that," Angeline said placidly. "Lots and lots of time."

By the summer of 1864, there were nearly three thousand residents in the community, and more than five hundred houses. The contrabands had built a sawmill for the army, and many of them were employed there. Others were hired by the army to repair the fort they had built and to work in the army mess. More and more of the men were starting their own small businesses. Some of the women, like Ella, continued to cook and do laundry for the soldiers.

But the army still owed them money, and people were beginning to complain more openly.

"The white soldiers gets their pay, you kin bet on that," Royall said.

"You heared they's cuttin' rations for the colored soldiers' wives and chilluns?" another man asked. "Cap'n wants to starve 'em to death, I reckon."

"Cap'n tole me I wouldn't get no more pay after I got shot," Royall said. "Tole me I was no more use to the army. That's why we gotta take care of our own selves. Cain't be 'spectin' the gov'ment to look out for us no more."

That spring and summer more teachers arrived from the North. Maddie was fearful that she wouldn't be needed to teach the little ones anymore, but Miss James reassured her. "With more than a thousand children on the island, Maddie, even a dozen teachers couldn't educate them all."

Schools were built around the island with lumber from the sawmill. And Miss James was right; Maddie was busier than ever with her teaching. She didn't see as much of Angeline now, but in most other ways life didn't change. Externally, at least.

But inside, Maddie felt different. Maybe it was because she was fourteen, in long skirts, and wearing her hair up. Or maybe it was because of the long, hard winter of missing Papa and fearing that Pride would die. Whatever the reason, Maddie no longer felt like a little girl.

Angeline was the first to remark on the change. She was visiting with Ella after supper one night, while Maddie put away the dishes.

"You look like a young lady now," Angeline said as she

watched her sister work. "And you're gettin' prettier ever' day. I'll bet our Zeb's noticed, too."

"Our Zeb's too busy puttin' food on the table and totin' shingles for your husband to notice much of anything," Maddie said tartly.

"Don't tell me you're still not ready for courtin'." Angeline turned to Ella. "Don't you think she's old enough to be seein' a young man, Mama?"

Ella looked up from her knitting. "I wouldn't stand in her way if Maddie wanted to step out with Zebedee, but that's up to her and Zeb."

"Don't you want a house of your own someday, Maddie?" Angeline persisted. "And a husband to take care of you?"

Ella chuckled. "If there was ever a person could take care of herself, it's Maddie."

Angeline frowned. "But, Mama, don't you want her to marry and have a family?"

"Family's the most important thing—the *only* thing—in my life," Ella said. "But Maddie'll have to decide what's most important to her."

Maddie wanted to run to her mama and hug her for those words. She had finally said that Maddie was fine just the way she was, that her feelings mattered.

Maddie wouldn't have admitted it to Angeline, but she *had* given some thought to marriage this past year. Sometimes she envied Angeline and Royall their happiness. And she thought Ella was the luckiest woman alive to have a man like Papa. But when she thought about marrying Zebedee, she couldn't begin to imagine it.

She cared about Zeb. Of course, she did! She worried about him joining the army; she fussed over him when he was sick. But was that kind of caring enough? She was pretty sure she didn't feel for Zebedee what Angeline felt for Royall. She sure didn't long for the day when they could share a home together. She wasn't even sure she wanted to share a home with any man. Because Maddie had other dreams.

She wanted to go to the North. She wanted to see the cities and the people that Miss James talked about. She wanted to learn everything about everything. And after the war was over—if it ever was over—she wanted to come back to North Carolina and teach, as Miss James was teaching her. What man—even a special man like Zebedee—would want his wife to do that? Now that she had tasted freedom, Maddie wasn't sure she could accept another kind of bondage—even from somebody who loved her.

Twenty-Five

It was a muggy day in July. Maddie was in Royall's workshop helping Zebedee crate piles of finished shingles. They had just finished when Angeline came to the door and told them to come outside for a piece of apple pie.

Maddie and Zebedee joined Royall under the old gum tree. They gratefully accepted the mugs of cold milk and slices of pie Angeline brought them.

"Zeb, I been thinkin'," Royall said. "Maybe you'd like to be my partner in the business. I kin teach you to split shingles."

"That's mighty nice'a you," Zebedee said slowly. "I'd be pleased to work with you, but I don't rightly see how I kin."

Royall looked surprised. "You got other plans?"

"Yessir, I does. I figger I've put it off long enough. It's about time for me to join the army."

Maddie stopped chewing and stared at Zebedee.

"Now, Maddie, don't go lookin' at me that way," the boy said softly.

"What you want me to do—wish you well on decidin' to get yourself killed?"

"Maddie, why don't you go help your sister?" Royall said gently.

"And leave you to fill this boy's head with the glories of

bein' a soldier?" Maddie demanded. "Uh-uhhh. I'm stayin'."

"Somebody else is gonna have to praise war to Zeb," Royall said. " 'Cause it's a terrible thing—nothin' like you expect."

"But you went," Zeb said.

"First off, I was older'n you. And if I'd knowed then what I knows now . . ." Royall shrugged. "I cain't say I wouldn't of gone, but I'd of thought about it a lot more'n I did."

"But you still went," Zebedee said stubbornly. "You did what a man's s'posed to do."

Royall frowned. "I pictured myself in that fine uniform, settin' 'round the fire the way the soldiers did here, sharin' stories and feelin' brave. But it wasn't like that."

"What was it like?" Maddie asked.

"Lonesome, mostly. I'd think about supper with all of us together, the sun risin' over the sound, the things you don't take notice of when you got 'em. Titus and me talked about home all the time. Helped to shut out what was happenin' 'round us. The dirt and the blood. The noise durin' the fightin'! Sometimes I thought them guns would drive me plumb crazy."

"But you got through it, and you come back home," Zebedee persisted.

"Barely. And lots'a men won't come back," Royall said. "I seen too many men die, Zeb. And it's a terrible death when a bullet rips through your gut and you lie there in the blood and stink for hours 'fore you die."

Maddie was thinking about her papa now. Alone and missing his family, in danger all the time. But he would be back—she prayed every night for that and believed that her prayers would be answered. She had to believe.

"Zeb, war's bad for any man," Royall went on, "but it's worse for a colored man. The white soldiers hates us—North or South, don't matter which side they's fightin' on, they'd just as soon see us die as not. Thinks we's uppity, tryin' to be as good as they is. The bluecoats don't *want* us in their army."

Zebedee's face was troubled. "But Titus sez we gotta be willin' to fight for our freedom."

"You're willin'," Royall said. "You just ain't old enough yet. Anyhow, from what I hear, this war cain't last much longer. Both sides is runnin' outta food and ammunition. It's windin' down now."

"Zeb, we need you more than the army does," Maddie said.

"Maddie's right, son," Royall said. "Why don't you wait and see if this war ain't nearly over?"

"Guess I kin wait a little while," Zebedee agreed reluctantly. "But if it don't end soon, I'm goin'."

The next Sunday before services Maddie heard folks complaining about the army again. How they still owed people money. How they were cutting rations more. How soldiers came to their houses at night and stole chickens and pigs and vegetables from their gardens. They spoke softly, afraid of being overheard, but Maddie caught the anger in their voices.

Brother Earl's sermon was about forgiveness. It was a real good sermon, Maddie thought, but the people around her seemed restless. Finally, a man called out, "I thinks we done forgive enough!"

Others joined in, grumbling their agreement.

"We's got men dyin' for the Union, and what does we get?" a woman demanded. "They not givin' me enough to keep my babies alive. I got a husband and a son in their army, and we ain't seen a cent yet. Don't tell me to forgive, Brother, 'cause I cain't!"

"I hears the army's sellin' our rations," another man said. "They's makin' money while our chilluns go without!"

"And they tole us we could have planks from the mill to build our houses—now they's sellin' 'em to us for four dollars a hundred. Who was it done built that mill? And who's got that kinda money?"

"*We'd* have it if they'd give us our back pay!"

"They don't treat us no different than our masters did—'cept they don't buy and sell us."

Brother Earl tried to calm them down, but the dam of fear had been broken. They were all calling out grievances now, demanding that Brother Earl do something about it.

"We'll write a letter to General Butler," Brother Earl told them. "After services today, I'll take down ever'thing you tells me. If the cap'n won't listen, we'll go to his superiors."

Somewhat mollified, the congregation quieted down. Brother Earl didn't try to finish his sermon. Instead, he led them in a song. It was Maddie's favorite hymn, because it was about freedom. The Jubilee!

Michael, haul the boat ashore,
Then you'll hear the horn they blow,
Then you'll hear the trumpet sound,
Trumpet sound the world around,
Trumpet sound for rich and poor,
Trumpet sound the Jubilee,
Trumpet sound for you and me.

They were pouring all their anger and hope into that hymn. Their voices swelled with passion and power. Then Maddie realized that some people had stopped singing.

She turned around to see what was happening and saw a half dozen young bluecoats sidling in, grinning and looking like they were up to no good.

The singing stopped altogether. Brother Earl stepped from behind the pulpit and extended his hand to the soldiers. "Welcome, brothers," he said. "We's glad you could be with us today. Won't you join us in a song'a praise to our Lord?"

"We ain't your brothers," one of the soldiers snapped. "And we ain't here to praise no heathen god'a yours."

"Just makin' sure you ain't causin' no trouble," another soldier said.

"Don't seem to be any trouble here," the first soldier remarked with a smirk. "Seems mighty quiet to me."

"Maybe too quiet." One of the soldiers walked down the center aisle toward Brother Earl. "I don't think your people got the spirit of the Lord in their hearts, preacher. Looks like they need sump'n to wake 'em up."

The soldier raised his arm and swung it toward the congregation. There was a streak of fire, then a series of small, rapid explosions. Somebody screamed. People scrambled from their seats, running from the noise and the cloud of smoke that drifted from the center of the crowd.

Maddie was running too, as best she could in the crush of bodies. A child fell under her feet. She stumbled, trying not to step on him.

Then somebody cried out, "It's just pop crackers! They done throwed pop crackers."

"Stay calm, brothers and sisters!" Brother Earl was yelling. "You hear that? It's just pop crackers. There's no danger!"

Silence descended over the congregation. Now they

could hear the soldiers snickering, see them bending over as their laughter grew and erupted into the stillness.

Maddie saw Brother Earl stoop down and pick up the charred remains of the soldiers' prank. He looked at the burned debris, then raised his eyes to the soldier nearest him. He had a look of fury on his face.

"We invite you in to worship with us," he said. "We welcome you as brothers, and you treat us like ignorant beasts. There's chilluns here, old folks, that could'a been trampled. Or scairt to death!"

The soldiers' laughter grew.

Brother Earl threw the burned firecrackers to the ground and started toward the soldiers.

"Stay where you are!" one of the soldiers ordered, no longer laughing. He pulled a pistol from his side and pointed it at Brother Earl, just inches from the preacher's chest.

"You take one more step," the soldier said, "and I pull the trigger."

The soldiers were angry now. They glared at the frightened faces around them.

Nobody spoke or moved. Finally the soldier lowered his pistol. "I'm sick and tired of you gettin' everything handed to you," he said. "And thinkin' you're as good as I am. I'd like to dump ever' last one'a you into the sound with a rock tied to your feet!"

"Come on, Hank, 'fore somebody comes," another soldier said. He was already edging away.

The one standing by Brother Earl swore an oath and turned to leave.

The congregation stayed where they were until the soldiers were gone. Then they gathered silently around Brother Earl.

"We gotta do sump'n," Doc said. "They's gettin' outta hand. We ain't safe in our own church."

The others murmured their agreement, but their earlier passion was gone.

"We'll report it to the cap'n," Brother Earl said. "Then we'll write General Butler."

Some nodded, but their shoulders sagged and their faces were weary. Nobody believed that talk or letters would change a thing.

Twenty-Six

Some six months after his illness, Pride still tired easily and couldn't put on weight. He was tall for five, and handsome, but so skinny that Ella fretted over him constantly.

"Just leave him be," Angeline said one afternoon when Ella had gone to the window a half dozen times to watch him playing in the yard. "He's growin' stronger ever' day."

"No, he's not," Ella said, but she returned to her sewing and didn't go near the window again.

In August, Pride started school. Maddie had been teaching him his letters at home, and he was already able to read simple passages. She was so proud of him the first time he stood in front of the class and read a whole paragraph aloud.

Like Maddie, Pride was fascinated by the written word. Every night he begged her for a story, and she'd read to him from the Bible or from one of the books Miss James had loaned her.

"Your papa's gonna be mighty proud of your readin' when he gets home," Ella told him.

Titus had been gone over a year now and Ella was afraid Pride might not remember him, so she spoke of him often. "Papa will like that story Maddie just read you," she would say. Or, "Your papa used to sit by the fire like you are now, rockin' you till you went to sleep."

Maddie knew what Ella was doing and shared her own memories of Titus with Pride. It helped her, too, to talk about him.

Maddie was outside playing a game of hide-the-switch with Pride one evening when Royall and Angeline came over. They greeted Maddie as they always did, and Royall teased Pride, but Maddie could sense something different about them. When they went into the house, Maddie scooped up Pride and followed.

It didn't take Maddie long to find out what was going on. They had barely sat down when Angeline told Ella that she was going to have a baby. Ella's face lit up like the candles on Mistress McCartha's Christmas tree.

"Sister Melba says we can plan on a winter baby," Angeline said. "Sometime in February."

"We'll have to start makin' warm little clothes," Ella said. Then she sighed. "Wish Aunt Lucy was here. She could always tell if it was a boy or a girl."

"We's gonna have lots'a both, so it really don't matter," Royall said.

"And whata you think about it, little man?" Ella asked a weary Pride as he climbed into her lap. "You're gonna be an uncle."

Curling up against her, Pride considered this. "What's an uncle?" he asked finally.

Everybody laughed, even Ella, but Maddie saw the shadow that crossed Ella's face when she looked down at her exhausted son.

A few weeks later, Maddie stopped by to see Angeline on her way home from school. Angeline seemed preoccupied. When they sat down to have coffee, Maddie said, "Is anythin' wrong? The baby?"

"No," Angeline said quickly. "I'm fine. It's just somethin' Royall told me last night, somethin' that happened when he was still in the army."

The look on Angeline's face frightened Maddie. "What did he tell you?"

"Royall said that Papa met up with some Yankee soldiers in Virginia. They'd just come up through North Carolina, and from what they said, Papa figured they'd come close to River Bend. When he described the house, they said yes, they'd seen it—right 'fore they burned it to the ground."

"Oh, Angeline, no!"

"Royall hadn't told me before 'cause he figgered I'd be upset," Angeline said. "And I was. 'Specially when I heard they'd burned the cabins too."

Maddie felt sick. "What happened to Aunt Lucy and Elsie and the others?"

Angeline shook her head. "I don't know. The men told Papa they saw some slaves runnin' off into the woods."

"Maybe they made it to a safe place up North."

"Some of the younguns, maybe, but Aunt Lucy and Luther couldn't go far."

"Mistress said they'd burn the house," Maddie said. Her voice was hard. "Reckon they stole all the food and animals too."

"Royall says that's what war's like," Angeline said gently. "Soldiers on both sides do what they have to."

"Why do they have to burn down old people's homes?" Maddie asked angrily. "Why the cabins, Angeline?"

Angeline just shook her head.

Maddie wrestled with her anger for days. She couldn't believe that men like Sergeant Taylor—and even her own papa—would hurt innocent people. But there were men on the island who enjoyed hurting folks. Like the ones who'd brought pop crackers to their church. Had she been wrong to think that white people up North really cared about the slaves? Were they any better than whites in the South?

Maddie was cleaning the chalkboard after school one day when Miss James asked to speak to her.

"Tell me what's bothering you." The teacher looked squarely into Maddie's eyes, making it impossible for her to look away.

"Nothin', ma'am."

"Nothing's the reason for that long face?" Miss James asked gently. "Are you worried about Pride?"

Maddie shook her head.

"Then what?"

Maddie wanted to share her confusion with this woman she admired so. But she was afraid. Would a lady from the North be shocked by her anger toward the Yankee soldiers? Would she think Maddie was disloyal? Ungrateful?

Finally her need to talk won out. She told Miss James about the cabins being burned, about her friends being left without homes.

"Some of the children are younger'n Pride. What did *they* do wrong?"

"They did nothing wrong." Miss James's voice was even, soft, as it always was. But her eyes were dark with anger. "Soldiers burn buildings so nothing will be left for the enemy to use. It's how armies win wars."

"My mistress used to say the Yankees were devils, but

my papa said they'd help us." Maddie hesitated, trying to sort it all out. "I thought Mistress was wrong. I thought all the Yankees would be like Sergeant Taylor. And you." Maddie dropped her eyes. "But most of 'em *are* devils. They hate us, don't they?"

"Some of them don't understand that one group of people is no better and no worse than any other group. What about your master and mistress? Were they all bad?"

"No," Maddie admitted. "They gave us plenty to eat. And Mistress taught Mama to read."

"Were they good in every way?"

Maddie thought of the ugly brand on Bertie's cheek. "No, ma'am, they surely weren't."

"Well, people from the North are like that too. Sometimes they're kind and generous. And sometimes they do terrible things. Because of ignorance. Or greed. Or because they're afraid of what they don't understand. But there *are* good people in the world, Maddie. And you'll know when you meet them."

Maddie never did tell Ella about River Bend. Neither did Angeline. It was their first serious secret, and it made Maddie feel even older. Like she was the mama now, instead of Ella.

A few days after her talk with Miss James, Maddie was helping Ella fix supper. Zebedee was reading Pride a story.

"Wonder what's keepin' Angeline and Royall," Ella said.

"Maybe she got held up at the hospital."

"I wish she'd quit workin' there now the baby's comin'."

Supper was on the table, and still Angeline and Royall

didn't come. Ella had just told Zebedee to run next door, when the front door opened. It was Royall, followed by Angeline.

Maddie knew the instant she saw Angeline's face. She didn't have to hear the words Royall was saying. Or hear Ella repeat them numbly. She *knew.*

"Titus?" Ella said again. "No, there's some mistake."

"No, Mama." Tears poured down Angeline's cheeks. "They're sure. Sergeant Taylor checked himself."

"Sergeant Taylor told you this?" Ella's voice was calm, too calm. Her eyes were stone dry.

"He thought it might be easier comin' from us," Angeline said. She began to sob and ran to embrace her mama. Ella accepted the arms around her passively. She just stood there, staring at nothing.

Maddie knew she should go to Ella. But she couldn't move or speak. She heard a roaring in her head—like the waves hitting the beach at Nags Head—and felt like she was drowning.

She felt Royall take her arm and lead her to a chair. She saw Pride's frightened face, and the wetness of Zebedee's eyes as they sought hers. She heard Angeline's sobs, and Royall's attempts to comfort. But it all seemed to be happening to somebody else. It wasn't real. It couldn't be. And yet, she knew it was.

"Where'd it happen?" Ella asked the emptiness.

"Tennessee."

"When?"

"Four months ago."

"Four months!" Ella flinched. "And I never knew." She turned anxiously to Angeline. "Shouldn't I have felt it when it happened?"

"I don't know, Mama," Angeline whispered.

"Where is he?"

"They buried him in Tennessee," Royall said.

Ella's body sagged. Royall helped Angeline support her.

"You mean, we can't even bury him?" Maddie had finally found her voice. But it was so weak, and Angeline was crying so hard, nobody heard her.

Twenty-Seven

September gave way to October, and it was suddenly cold again. Nearly a month had passed since the family had learned that Titus was dead. Struggling with the pain of her own grief, Maddie marveled at Ella's courage, even while it worried her. Ella never cried, and she never spoke of Titus after that first terrible day.

"She should talk about it, like we do," Maddie said to Angeline one afternoon as they sat in Angeline's kitchen. "If she keeps it all inside, she's gonna burst one day."

"I wish she'd talk too. But we all handle our pain in our own way. Just look at you," Angeline said. "I cry my eyes out ever' day, and I haven't seen you shed a tear."

Maddie thought about this. It was true she hadn't cried for Papa. Her pain was real enough; it kept her from eating and sleeping and reading the books Miss James gave her. But her papa's death didn't seem real. She hadn't seen him die—they didn't even know where his grave was—so a part of her believed, *hoped*, that it was a mistake. That Papa was still alive and would be coming home. Maybe Mama believed that too.

"Only time she brightens up is when we mention the baby." Angeline patted the little bulge in her middle. "Royall and I were talkin' about namin' it Titus if it's a boy. You think that'd cause Mama pain?"

"I think she'd be proud." Maddie felt a heavy stone settle against her ribs. "When you gonna tell her?"

"Not till the baby comes. If it's a girl, we'll call her Ella. How you like Ella Henry Tate?"

"I like it just fine," Maddie said. She hoped it would be a girl. She wasn't ready to see Papa's name given to somebody else, even his own grandbaby.

Maddie worked hard at trying to bring a smile to her mama's somber face. And since Angeline was right—that her expected grandbaby was the only thing that seemed to engage Ella—Maddie talked a lot about the baby that autumn. Even Zebedee joined in by thinking up silly names for the child. "How about Huckleberry Henry Tate, Miz Ella?" he'd say suddenly. "You like that better than Spider Lily?"

Maddie didn't know what she would have done without Zeb. It wasn't that he said or did anything special; he was just there, ready to listen when she felt most empty and alone. And she knew that he had loved her papa, too, so she was able to share her grief with him. But still, she couldn't cry.

At least Zebedee had stopped talking about joining the army, Maddie was relieved to see. With Royall not fully recovered and Titus not coming back, Zeb thought of himself as the man of the family. He worked harder than ever to see that they were well fed and that repairs were made to the house. Maddie noticed that he was spending more time with Pride, too, showing him how to set traps and mend tools, as a father would show his son.

Maddie didn't have the heart to read aloud in the evenings, but she still helped Pride with his schoolwork and told him stories. The Walt Whitman book was tucked away in a corner of her clothes cupboard. Maddie couldn't bring herself to look at it. Rather than bringing her joy, as it had in the past, it was now just another painful reminder of what she had lost.

School still brought Maddie her greatest moments of peace. When she was teaching the children, or learning about a foreign land from Miss James, she could forget for a while the wearying sadness that she carried with her day and night.

On one especially fine October day, when the chill of approaching winter had retreated for a time and the sun was unusually bright, Maddie finished her chores at school and started for home. On impulse, she turned off the path and headed for the little cemetery where her people were buried.

There were many graves now, several too new to have grown a covering of grass and vines. All the graves faced east and were encircled with rings of shells from the ocean. Sister Melba had told her the shells were there to protect the dead from evil spirits. And the graves faced the direction of the rising sun because that was where the door to Heaven lay.

It was a beautiful place to rest after laying aside life's burdens, Maddie thought. So quiet and protected by the forest from the cares of everyday life. The leaves had turned, shining orange, gold, and crimson in the sunlight. Soon the graves would be covered with them, a brilliant patchwork like the quilts Ella made.

Maddie didn't know why she had come here, except that she longed for a place where she could feel closer to her papa—where she could talk to him, and hope that he would hear. Sister Melba said the spirits of the dead return to where they were most happy in life, to where their people are. Maddie wanted to believe that her papa's spirit had come back to the island.

She tried to feel his presence in the silent cemetery. And she talked to him. About Angeline's baby and Pride's reading and Royall's mending leg. But, still, there was an emptiness inside her. She could feel nothing of the strong, loving man who had been her papa.

She had turned with a heavy heart to leave the cemetery when she saw the flock of birds in the eastern sky. They were flying from the North, great white birds with a touch of black on their outstretched wings. The last of the snow geese coming to Pea Island for the winter.

Maddie stood with her head thrown back, eyes shaded by her hand, watching their graceful flight. She was lost in the memory of one autumn morning when she and Titus had stood outside their tent enjoying the sight of a thousand such birds soaring across the sky. The stone in her chest shifted. Suddenly she felt the most searing pain she had ever known. And the tears that had refused to come were welling in her eyes, blurring the image of the birds, pouring down her cheeks in salty rivers.

She cried out. It was the sound of hurt surprise that a small animal makes when it steps into a human trap. She slid to the ground, limp as the cotton-filled dolls that Ella had made for her long ago. And she cried.

The idea came to her slowly. She began to dig in the earth with her fingers, breathing in the musky odors of damp soil and rotting leaves. She dug and dug, until she had a small hill of sand at her knees. She patted and molded the hill until it resembled, in miniature, the grave mounds around it. Then she gathered shells from nearby graves and began to lay them around the base of the hill she had made.

She was so preoccupied she didn't realize she was no longer alone until she heard leaves crackling underfoot as someone drew near. Resentment at the intrusion showed on Maddie's face when she looked up—and saw Miss James standing there.

The teacher stood over Maddie for a moment, her back to the sun, her face hidden in shadow. Then she turned away without speaking and went to one of the graves. Maddie watched as Miss James picked up several shells, brought them back, and held them out to her.

They worked together in silence. Miss James collected the shells, and Maddie arranged them carefully. After a while the pain in Maddie's chest began to ease a little. The tears still poured, falling on the ground and on the shells and on the teacher's hands when she returned with her offerings.

They still hadn't spoken when the shells were all in place and they sat back to look at their work. Maddie wasn't sure how long she stayed there or when Miss James slipped away. But the sun had disappeared behind the trees when Maddie finally struggled to her feet—and turning to go, told her papa good-bye.

Twenty-Eight

"Mama, how many pies for Christmas?" Angeline asked. She and Royall were spending the evening at Ella's house. As usual, Ella was saying very little.

"Whatever you think," Ella said. She didn't look up from the quilt she was piecing.

Pride coughed, a deep, raspy cough. Ella looked anxiously toward the table where he was doing his lessons. The dreaded fevers had come back with the first cold weather.

"Martha's too crippled to bake anymore," Angeline said quickly. "I'll tell her we'll do it all this year."

"You shouldn't be on your feet with your time so close," Ella said.

Maddie looked at her sister, who was now plump and round. "I'll help."

Ella studied her older daughter's belly with knowing eyes. "That's a boy you're carryin'. Too high to be a girl."

"But Sister Melba says if it kicks to the left—"

"I don't care what Sister Melba says," Ella interrupted Royall. "I carried the boy babies just that way. Angeline and Maddie was lower."

Encouraged by her mama's sudden show of spirit, Angeline went back to plans for Christmas dinner. Maddie joined in, even though her heart wasn't in it. Last Christmas had been dreary with Papa not here, but this year . . . Rather than think about it, she went to see if she could help Pride with his lessons.

They did their best to make the holiday joyful for Pride's sake, but everybody was secretly glad when Christmas had come and gone. The celebrations going on around them only reminded them more sharply of their own heavy hearts. And then they all worried about Pride.

He was not as ill as he had been the previous winter, but he often woke in the night with fever and chills. By late December, Ella was keeping him in the house. Most days he didn't have the strength to complain, but some mornings he fussed so loudly over missing school, they had hope that he was getting better. Then he would become lifeless again.

"Pride just has to get better," Maddie said to Angeline and Zebedee day after day. "If anything happens to him now . . ."

She didn't need to finish. They all knew she was thinking that Ella couldn't stand another loss so soon after Titus.

Maddie knew that she would grieve for Titus for a long time, but she also knew that she was strong enough to accept the loss and go on. She wasn't so sure about Ella. "Take care of your mama," Aunt Lucy had said that day so long ago. And Maddie tried.

By January Pride's breathing was so labored that Maddie set up a sleeping tent for him. She draped a blanket over his bed, covering him from head to foot, and placed a kettle of steaming water inside to help him breathe. Sometimes she sat with Ella beside his bed all night, applying poultices and singing songs.

Pride was having an especially bad time the night Royall came to tell them that Angeline's baby was coming. Ella's sudden joy was short-lived. She was torn between being there when her first grandchild came into the world and staying with her ill son.

"Go to Angeline," Maddie said. "I'll send Zebedee if Pride gets worse."

"But Angeline has Sister Melba." Ella bent to stroke her son's hot face.

"She wants you there," Maddie said. "Pride's asleep. He won't know you're gone. Go be with your daughter, Mama."

When Ella got to Angeline's house, Sister Melba was already there. She had stuffed rags into cracks under the doors to keep out evil spirits, and had placed an ax under Angeline's bed to cut the pain, but a dull one so that the mother wouldn't bleed too much. Royall was hovering anxiously outside the closed door of their bedroom.

Angeline was sitting up in bed when Ella came in. She greeted her mama cheerfully.

"So far, it's not so bad," Angeline said. Then a spasm of pain gripped her and she fell back on the pillows.

"Won't be a long birthin'," Sister Melba told Ella. "The girl's doin' fine."

Ella went to her daughter's bedside to see for herself.

It was nearly dawn when the baby was born.

"It's a girl child," Ella whispered to Angeline. She wiped her daughter's glistening face.

"A girl," Angeline repeated weakly. She smiled as she sought out the squalling bundle in the healer's arms. "Is she strong?"

"Strong as kin be." Sister Melba folded a blanket around the baby and placed her in Angeline's arms.

"How tiny she is," Angeline said softly as she peered into the little face.

Ella's eyes filled. "She's a pretty one, daughter."

Angeline looked up at her mama, her face glowing. "Royall and I decided, if the baby was a girl, we wanted to name her after you. Ella Henry—"

"No!"

Sister Melba's screech startled Ella and Angeline. The baby started to cry again.

"Don't you know not to speak the child's name 'fore the ninth day after the birthin'?"

Ella and Angeline exchanged looks.

"If you name the child 'fore the chance of nine-day fever's passed, she'll die."

"Don't even say such a thing," Ella said. She touched her granddaughter's tiny fist as though to assure herself that the child was well. "This baby's strong and healthy."

"Won't be if you calls her Ella," Sister Melba warned. "You'll have to wait and name her again."

"In all my days, I never heard such a thing," Ella muttered.

"I wanted to name her after you, Mama." Angeline studied her child with worried eyes.

"Well, you cain't," the healer said. "And that's that."

Maddie stopped by on her way home from school one day and found her sister rocking the baby and singing to her.

"You're spoilin' that child," Maddie said. "She won't ever learn to walk the way you hold on to her."

"Can't spoil a child by lovin' it," Angeline said serenely. "I understand now why family means everythin' to Mama."

"Too bad you couldn't call her Ella."

"Mama said, 'That woman's touched in the head, but no use takin' chances.' "

"Anyhow, Miss James is pleased you named her Elizabeth."

"That was Mama's doin' too. She said our baby should be named for a free-born woman. Lord knows, I don't know that many free-born women—and I wasn't about to call her Althea for the Mistress."

Maddie smiled. "No, that would never do."

"Mama seems better."

Maddie nodded, then laughed as the infant opened her tiny mouth and yawned mightily. "This little girl has a lot to do with it."

"Don't you want one just like her someday?" Angeline thrust the blanketed bundle into Maddie's arms.

Maddie lay her cheek against the side of Elizabeth's head. She breathed in the sweet baby scent and a wave of tenderness washed over her. "Maybe."

Angeline shook her head. "You always were the most peculiar child."

Maddie found herself repeating the conversation to Ella that evening. "I suppose I *was* peculiar," she said.

"You were different from Angeline," Ella said. "I never worried a minute about her, and nearly fretted myself sick over you. But your papa said, 'Give her time to find her way, Ella. She'll make you just as proud as Angeline does.' " Ella looked up from the sock she was darning. "And you have, Maddie."

There was a comfortable silence. Then Ella said, "I have a confession to make, somethin' I've been frettin' over a long time."

"What is it, Mama?"

"I told you once I'd never trust you again. You don't know how sorry I am for sayin' that."

"Mama, it's all right," Maddie said quickly. She was startled, elated, and embarrassed all at the same time. They were careful not to look at each other for a moment.

"You were as important in Pride's healin' as I was—prob'ly more," Ella said. "I just want you to know—I'd trust you with him the same as I'd trust myself."

A few days later, Zebedee came home with word that the war was over.

"The soldiers sez the South ain't surrendered yet, but it's good as done." He let out a whoop. "Means slaves ever'wheres gonna be free."

"Hope your papa knows," Ella said to Maddie.

"He knows." And Maddie believed he did.

"Reckon this means we don't have to worry about bein' kicked off our land," Royall said.

"I'll believe it when the South says 'Enough!'" Ella said. But she was smiling.

Twenty-Nine

A few days later Maddie learned to fully appreciate the caution that had guided Ella all her life. She was sitting outside Angeline's house with Ella, Angeline, and Pride, with baby Elizabeth asleep in her lap. Sergeant Taylor was coming down the street. He cut across Ella's yard and made straight for them.

"Come to say good-bye," he said. "I'm goin' home."

"You won't be back?" Maddie asked.

He shook his head. "They tell me I'm too old to shoulder a rifle, so I'm gettin' out."

He didn't look happy about it, Maddie thought. And there was something else—the way he wouldn't look at them, just kept frowning at his feet—that made her uneasy.

"Thank you for all you've done for me and my family, Sergeant," Ella said.

His frown spread. "I don't deserve your thanks, 'specially now." He turned to stare out over the trees behind Angeline's house. "There's talk the government's gonna ask you folks to leave the island."

"That can't be." Angeline's voice was soft but firm. "They gave us the land."

"I know what they did. But they're already grantin' pardons to the men who owned this land. With a pardon, they'll get it back."

There was a look of panic in Angeline's eyes. "But this was just wilderness 'fore we came. Our homes and businesses—how can you make us leave 'em?"

"Daughter, the sergeant's just tellin' us. It's not his fault," Ella said. Maddie was amazed by Ella's apparent calm. Did she understand what the sergeant was saying?

"You're sure about this?" Ella asked.

Sergeant Taylor nodded. "I'm sorry."

"We'll fight it," Angeline said. "Won't we, Mama? We won't go."

The sergeant turned to Maddie. "Keep readin' your books, young lady. They need teachers other places 'sides here."

Maddie nodded. She wanted to thank him—for the Christmas book and the slates, and for being their friend. But he was gone before she could find the words.

Over supper that night, Royall said, "Maybe the sergeant don't know what he's talkin' about."

"That's right," Angeline said. "They can't just take our land and tell us to go."

"The men that owned this land are white," Ella said. "You think a government of white men is gonna keep 'em off their land for the sake of some slaves?"

Royall's eyes flashed. "We ain't slaves no more. We's equal to the white man."

Ella didn't say anything, but Maddie could see the sadness in her face. And the resignation.

"Doc and the others don't believe it," Royall went on. "They sez they ain't goin' nowhere."

"Neither am I," Angeline said. "Think how hard it would be—movin' away with a baby."

"And who told you this life would be easy?" Ella asked. She looked at Angeline with love and pity in her eyes. "I wanted a safe life for my children. I wanted it so much, I was scared'a livin'. But your papa—he knew better. He knew that sometimes you gotta just grab hold'a whatever's scarin' you and face up to it. If we have to face up to leavin' the island, Angeline, we'll do it."

"We still got most'a the money from buildin' the fort," Royall said. "And the army pay."

Angeline turned anxious eyes to him. "You sayin' we should go? Just walk away from our home and everythin' we've worked for?"

"I'm sayin' if we *have* to, we'll have some money. I hear land's cheap now."

"But we don't know what it's like off the island," Angeline said. "I'm scared, Mama. What if they don't want us out there either?"

"Some won't," Ella said. "But maybe some will. We'll just have to see."

The war ended on the ninth of April, when General Lee surrendered to General Grant at Appomattox Courthouse. The Henrys and their neighbors cried tears of joy when they heard about the surrender. Children ran up and down the streets shouting and laughing and beating on tin plates. Grown-ups gathered to embrace one another and praise the Lord.

"Trumpet sound the jubilee," they sang. "Trumpet sound for you and me."

Maddie knew she would remember the feelings of that day for as long as she lived. The gladness and the wonder and—yes, the sadness of it.

* * *

One day in late May, Maddie helped Royall and Zebedee load the little boat that would take them away from Roanoke Island. Most of their friends were staying. They heard rumors every day that the army meant to force them off the land, but they refused to believe it. How could they leave their homes? they asked. What would they do away from the island? Where would they go?

Maddie and her family were moving to the mainland, to look for land they could buy and farm. After she had helped the others make a new home for themselves, Maddie meant to go North. But there was time for that. Plenty of time.

The sun was just peeking up over the pines as they boarded the boat. It was going to be a beautiful day.

Maddie was taking a last look at the island when Ella asked if she'd remembered to pack the book of poems. Maddie dug into the bundle of clothes at her feet and pulled it out.

"Read to us, daughter," Ella said. "Read us the one your papa liked."

Maddie opened the book and began to read.

Allons! we must not stop here,
However sweet these laid-up stores, however convenient this
*   dwelling we cannot remain here,*
However shelter'd this port and however calm these waters we
*   must not anchor here,*
However welcome the hospitality that surrounds us we are
*   permitted to receive it but a little while.*

Allons! the inducements will be greater,
We will sail pathless and wild seas,

We will go where winds blow, waves dash, and the Yankee clipper speeds by under full sail.

As the little boat left Roanoke Island far behind, Maddie's voice carried across the water. And as she read, she wondered ... wherever Papa was at that moment, was he listening?

Afterword

In 1865, the land on Roanoke Island was restored to those original owners who had received pardons. Many of the freed slaves who had made their homes there refused to leave. In November of 1866, 1,700 of them remained. The army was ordered to force them off the land they believed to be their own.

It was a sad ending to what had begun with such high hopes. But for the people who had made their way to Roanoke Island during the war years, the benefits had been many: They had been sheltered from the worst of the conflict and had earned enough money to help them resettle after the war was over. In addition, they had learned skills to ease their transition into a different society than the one they had known under slavery.

Some of the residents of the Roanoke Island community settled elsewhere on the Outer Banks, where they made their living from fishing and oystering. But most moved inland, to cities and towns in North Carolina where they could earn a better wage.

Some of the people did go up North, as Maddie dreamed of doing. Some did continue their educations. And some even returned to the South, to share with their brothers and sisters all that they had learned.